CARRYING THE SPANIARD'S CHILD

BY
JENNIE LUCAS

MILLS & BOON

First Published in Great Britain 2017
By Mills & Boon, an imprint of HarperCollins*Publishers*
1 London Bridge Street, London, SE1 9GF

© 2017 Jennie Lucas

ISBN: 978-0-263-92458-9

Printed and bound in Spain
by CPI, Barcelona

USA TODAY bestselling author **Jennie Lucas**'s parents owned a bookstore and she grew up surrounded by books, dreaming about faraway lands. A fourth-generation Westerner, she went east at sixteen to boarding school on scholarship, wandered the world, got married, then finally worked her way through college before happily returning to her hometown. A 2010 RITA® Award finalist and 2005 Golden Heart® Award winner, she lives in Idaho with her husband and children.

Books by Jennie Lucas

Mills & Boon Modern Romance

Uncovering Her Nine Month Secret
The Sheikh's Last Seduction
To Love, Honour and Betray
A Night of Living Dangerously
The Virgin's Choice

One Night With Consequences

The Consequence of His Vengeance
A Ring for Vincenzo's Heir
Nine Months to Redeem Him

Wedlocked!

Baby of His Revenge

To my husband, my own fairy-tale hero.

CHAPTER ONE

BELLE LANGTRY HAD hated Santiago Velazquez from the moment she'd laid eyes on him.

Well, not the *exact* moment, of course. She was only human. When they'd first met at their friends' wedding last September—Belle had been the maid of honor, Santiago the best man—she'd been dazzled by his dark gorgeousness, his height, his broad shoulders and muscular body. She'd looked up at his dark soulful eyes and thought, *Wow. Dreams really do come true.*

Then Santiago had turned to the groom and suggested out loud that Darius could still "make a run for it" and abandon his bride at the altar. And he'd said it right in front of Letty!

The bride and groom had awkwardly laughed it off, but from that moment, Belle had hated Santiago with a passion. Every word he said was more cynical and infuriating than the last. Within ten minutes, the two of them were arguing; by the end of the wedding, Belle wished he would do the world a favor and die. Being the forthright woman she was, she couldn't resist telling him so. He'd responded with sarcasm. And that had been their relationship for the last four months.

So of course, Belle thought bitterly, he would be the one to find her now, pacing the dark, snowy garden behind Letty and Darius's coastal estate. Crying.

Shivering in her thin black dress, she'd been looking

toward the wild Atlantic Ocean in the darkness. The rhythmic roar of the waves matched the thrumming of her heart.

All day, Belle had held her friend's adorable newborn as Letty wept through her father's funeral. By the end of the evening reception, the pain in Belle's heart as she held the sweetly sleeping baby had overwhelmed her. Gently giving the baby back to Letty, she'd mumbled an excuse and fled into the dark snow-covered garden.

Outside, an icy wind blew, freezing the tears against Belle's chapped skin as she stared out into the darkness, heartsick with grief.

She would never have a child of her own.

Never, the ocean sighed back to her. *Never, never.*

"Belle?" a rough voice called. "Are you out here?"

Santiago! She sucked in her breath. The last man she'd ever want to see her like this!

She could only imagine the arrogant sneer on the Spaniard's face if he found her crying over her inability to have a child. Ducking behind a frost-covered tree, she held her breath, praying he wouldn't see her.

"Belle, stop trying to hide," he said, sounding amused. "Your dress is black, and you're standing in the snow."

Gritting her teeth, she stepped out from behind the tree and lied, "I wasn't hiding."

"What are you doing out here, then?"

"I just needed some fresh air," she said desperately, wishing he'd leave her alone.

A beam of light from a second-floor window of the manor house illuminated the hard lines of Santiago's powerful body in the black suit and well-cut cashmere coat. As their eyes met, electricity coursed through her.

Santiago Velazquez was too handsome, she thought with an unwilling shiver. Too sexy. Too powerful. Too rich.

He was also a selfish, cynical playboy, whose only loyalty was to his own vast fortune. He probably had vaults big enough to swim in, she thought, and pictured him doing a backstroke through hundred-dollar bills. In the meantime he mocked the idea of kindness and respect. She'd heard he treated his one-night stands like unpaid employees. Belle's expression hardened. Folding her arms, she waited as he strode through the snow toward her.

He stopped a few feet away. "You don't have a coat."

"I'm not cold."

"I can hear your teeth chattering. Are you trying to freeze to death?"

"Why do you care?"

"Me? I don't," he said mildly. "If you want to freeze to death, it's fine with me. But it does seem selfish to force Letty to plan yet another funeral. So tedious, funerals. And weddings. And christenings. All of it."

"Any human interaction that involves emotion must be tedious to you," Belle said.

He was nearly a foot taller than her own petite height. His shoulders were broad and he wore arrogance like a cloak that shadowed him in the snow. She'd heard women call him Ángel, and she could well understand the nickname. He had a face like an angel—a dark angel, she thought irritably, if heaven needed a bouncer to keep lesser people out and boss everyone around. Santiago might be rich and handsome but he was also the most cynical, callous, despicable man on earth. He was everything she hated most.

"Wait." His black eyes narrowed as he stared down at her in the faint crystalline moonlight frosting the clouds. "Are you crying, Belle?"

She blinked hard and fast to hide the evidence. "No."

"You are." His cruel, sensual lips curved mockingly. "I know you have a pathetically soft heart, but this is pushing the limits even for you. You barely knew Letty's father, and yet here I find you mourning him after the funeral, alone in the snow like a tragic Victorian madwoman."

Normally that would have gotten a rise out of her. But not today. Belle's heart was too sad. And she knew if she showed the slightest emotion he'd only mock her more. Wishing desperately that Santiago hadn't been the one to find her, she said, "What do you want?"

"Darius and Letty have gone to bed. Letty wanted to come out and look for you but the baby needed her. I'm supposed to show you to your guest room and turn on the house alarm once you're brought in safe and sound."

His husky, Spanish-accented voice seemed to be laughing at her. She hated how, even disliking him as much as she did, he made her body shiver with awareness.

"I changed my mind about staying here tonight." The last thing she wanted was to spend the night tossing and turning in a guest room, with no company but her own agonizing thoughts. "I just want to go home."

"To Brooklyn?" Santiago looked at her incredulously. "It's too late. Everyone wanting to get back to the city left hours ago. The ice storm just closed the expressway. It might not reopen for hours."

"Why are you even still here? Don't you have a helicopter and a couple of planes? It can't be because you actually care about Letty and Darius."

"The guest rooms here are nice and I'm tired. Two days ago I was in Sydney. Before that, Tokyo." He yawned. "Tomorrow I leave for London."

"Poor you," said Belle, who had always dreamed of traveling but never managed to save the money, even for an economy ticket.

His sensual lips curved upward. "I appreciate your sympathy. So if you don't mind wrapping up your self-indulgent little *Wuthering Heights* routine I'd like to show you to your room so I can go to mine."

"If you want to go, go." She turned away so he couldn't see her exhausted, tearstained expression. "Tell Letty I'd already left. I'll get a train back to the city."

"Are you serious?" He looked down at her skeptically. "How will you reach the station? I doubt trains are even running—"

"Then I'll walk!" Her voice was suddenly shrill. "I'm not sleeping here!"

Santiago paused.

"Belle," he said, in a voice more gentle than she'd ever heard from him before. "What's wrong?"

Reaching out, he put his hand on her shoulder, then lifted it to her cheek. It was the first time he had ever touched her, and even in the dark and cold the touch of his hand spun through her like a fire. Her lips parted.

"If something was wrong, why would I tell you?"

His smile increased. "Because you hate me."

"And?"

"So whatever it is, you can tell me. Because you don't give a damn what I think."

"True," she said wryly. It was tempting. She pressed her lips together. "But you might tell the world."

"Do I ever share secrets?"

"No," she was forced to admit. "But you do say mean and insulting things. You are heartless and rude and..."

"Only to people's faces. Never behind their backs." His voice was low. "Tell me, Belle."

Clouds covered the moon, and they were briefly flooded in darkness. She suddenly was desperate to share her grief with someone, anyone. And it was true she couldn't have a lower opinion of him. He probably couldn't think less of her, either.

That thought was oddly comforting. She didn't have to pretend with Santiago. She didn't have to be positive and hopeful at all times, the cheerleader who tried to please everyone, no matter what. Belle had learned at a young age never to let any negative feelings show. If you were honest about your feelings, it only made people dislike you. It only made people leave, even and especially the ones you loved.

So Santiago was the only one she *could* tell. The only one she could be truly herself with. Because, heck, if he permanently left her life, she'd throw a party.

She took a deep breath. "It's the baby."

"Little Howie?"

"Yes."

"I had a hard time with him, too. Babies." He rolled his eyes. "All those diapers, all that crying. But what can you do? Some people still seem to want them."

"I do." The moon broke through the clouds, and Belle looked up at him with tears shimmering in the moonlight. "I want a baby."

He stared down at her, then snorted. "Of course you do. Romantic idiot like you. You want love, flowers, the whole package." He shrugged. "So why cry over it? If you are foolish enough to want a family, go get one. Settle down, buy a house, get married. No one is stopping you."

"I...I can't get pregnant," she whispered. "Ever. It's impossible."

"How do you know?"

"Because..." Belle looked down at the tracks in the snow. The moonlight caused strange shadows, mingling her footsteps and his. "I just know. It's medically impossible."

She braced herself for his inevitable questions. Medically impossible how? What happened? When and why?

But he surprised her.

Reaching out, he just pulled her into his arms, beneath his black cashmere coat. She felt the sudden comfort of his warmth, his strength, as he caressed her long dark hair. "Everything will be all right."

She looked up at him, her heart in her throat. She was aware of the heat of his body against hers.

"You must think I'm a horrible person," she said, pulling away. "A horrible friend for envying Letty, when she just lost her father. I spent all day holding her sweet baby and envying her. I'm the worst friend in the world."

"Stop." Cupping her face, he looked down at her fiercely. "You know I think you're a fool…existing in a pink cloud of candy-coated dreams. Someday you will lose those rose-colored glasses and learn the truth about the heartless world…"

She whispered brokenly. "I—"

He put his finger on her lips. "But even I can see you're a good friend."

His finger felt warm against her tingling lips. She had the sudden shocking desire to kiss it, to wrap her lips around his finger and suck it gently. She'd never had such a shocking thought before—she, an inexperienced virgin! But as little as she liked him, something about the wickedly sexy Spaniard attracted —and scared—her.

Trembling, she twisted her head away. She remembered all those women he'd famously seduced, those women she'd scorned as fools for being willing notches on his bedpost. And for the first time, she sympathized with them, as she herself fully felt the potent force of his charm.

"You're lucky, actually." Santiago gave her a crooked half grin. "Babies? Marriage? Who would want to be stuck with such a thankless responsibility as a family?" He shook his head. "No good would have come of it. It's a prison sentence. Now you can have something better."

She stared at him. "Better than a family?"

He nodded.

"Freedom," he said quietly.

"But I don't want freedom." Her voice was small. "I want to be loved."

"We all want things we can't have," he said roughly.

"How would you know? You've never wanted anything, not without taking it."

"You're wrong. There has been something I've wanted. For four months. Someone. But I can't have her."

Four months. Suddenly, Belle's heart was beating wildly in her chest. He couldn't mean…couldn't possibly mean…

Could Santiago Velazquez, the famous New York billionaire, a man who had supermodels for the asking, really want *Belle*—a plump, ordinary waitress from small-town Texas?

Their eyes held in the moonlight. Sparks ran through her body, from her earlobes to her hair to her breasts to the soles of her feet.

"I want her. I can't have her," he said in a low voice. "Not even if she were standing in front of me now."

"Why not?" she breathed.

"Ah." His lips twisted. "She wants love. I see it in her face. I hear it in her voice. She craves love like the air she breathes. If I took her, if I made her mine, she would turn all her romantic longings on me. And be destroyed by it." He looked down at her, his eyes dark and deep. "Because as much as I want her body, I do not want her heart."

Behind the soft silver halo on his black hair, she could dimly see the shadow of the manor house, and hear the ocean waves pounding on the unseen shore.

Then Belle's eyes suddenly narrowed.

He was playing with her, she realized. *Toying* with her. Like a sharp-clawed cat with a mouse. "Stop it."

"What?"

She lifted her chin. "Are you bored, Santiago? Do you want some company in your bed and I'm the only one around?" She glared at him. "Other women might fall for your world-weary playboy act. But I don't believe a word of it. If you really wanted me, you wouldn't let anything stand in the way, not my feelings and certainly not the risk of hurting me. You would seduce me without conscience. That's what a playboy does. So obviously, you don't want me. You're just bored."

"You're wrong, Belle." Roughly, he pulled her against his body, beneath his expensive black cashmere coat. She felt his warmth as his dark eyes searched hers hungrily. "I've wanted you since Darius and Letty's wedding. Since the first time you told me to go to hell." His sensual lips curved as he cupped her cheek and looked down at her intently. "But whatever you think of me, I'm not in the business of purposefully making naïve young women love me."

Her whole body was tingling with energy, with fear, with a feeling that could only be desire. She fought it desperately.

"You think I'd immediately fall in love with you?"

"Yes."

She gave an incredulous snort. "You have no problems with your ego, do you?"

His dark gaze seared her. "Tell me I'm wrong."

"You're wrong." She gave a careless shrug. "I do want love, it's true. If I met a man I could respect and admire, I might easily fall in love. But that's not you, Santiago." She looked at him evenly. "No matter how rich or sexy you might be. So if you want me, too bad. I don't want you."

His expression changed. His eyes glittered in the moonlight.

"You don't?" Reaching out, he ran his thumb lightly against her trembling bottom lip and whispered, "Are you sure?"

"Yes," she breathed, unable to pull away, or to look from his dark gaze.

He ran his hand down her arm, looking down at her as

if she were the most beautiful, desirable creature on earth. "And if I took you to my bed, you wouldn't fall in love?"

"Not even remotely. I think you're a total bastard."

But even as she spoke, Belle couldn't stop herself from shivering. She knew he felt it. The corners of his lips twisted upward in grim masculine satisfaction.

Softly, he ran his hand down through her hair. Her body's shivering intensified. As she breathed in his scent of sandalwood and firelight, she felt the strength and power of his body against hers, beneath his long black coat.

"Then there's no reason to hold back. Forget love." He gently lifted her chin. "Forget regret, forget pain, forget everything fate has denied you. For one night, take pleasure in what you can have, right here and now."

"You mean, take pleasure in you?"

She'd tried to say the words sarcastically, but the way her heart was hammering in her chest, her tone came out wrong. Instead of sarcastic, she sounded breathless. Yearning.

"For one night, let me give you joy. Without strings. Without consequences. Stop thinking so much about the future," he said in a low voice, his hand cupping her cheek. "For one night, you can know what it feels like to be truly, recklessly alive."

His black eyes seared hers, and the cold January night sizzled like west Texas in July as an arc of electricity passed between them.

Give herself to him for one night, without consequences? Without strings?

Belle stared up at him, shocked.

She'd never slept with anyone. She'd never even gotten close. She was, in fact, a twenty-eight-year-old virgin, an old maid who'd spent her whole life taking care of others, while failing to achieve a single dream for herself.

No. Her answer was no. Of course it was.

Wasn't it?

He didn't give her a chance to answer. Lowering his head, he kissed her cheek, his lips lingering against her skin, moving slowly. Sensuously. She held her breath, and as he drew back, she stared at him with big eyes, her whole body clamoring and clanging like an orchestra.

"All right," she heard herself say, then gasped at her own recklessness. She opened her mouth to take it back. Then stopped.

For one night, you can know what it feels like to be truly, recklessly alive.

When was the last time she'd felt that way?

Had she ever?

Or had she always been a good girl, trying so hard to please others, to follow the rules, to plan out her life?

What had being good ever done for her—except leave her heartsick and alone?

Santiago's dark eyes gleamed as he saw her hesitate. He didn't wait. Wrapping his large hands on her jawline and then sliding them to tangle in her hair, he slowly drew his mouth to hers. She felt the warmth of his breath, sweet like Scotch, against the tender flesh of her skin.

His sensual mouth lowered on hers, hot and demanding, pushing her lips apart. She felt the delicious sweep of his tongue, and the cold winter air between them heated to a thousand degrees.

She'd never been kissed like this before. Never. The tepid caresses she'd endured seven years ago were nothing compared to this ruthlessly demanding embrace, this—dark fire.

She was lost in his arms, in the hot demand of his mouth, of his hands everywhere. Desire swept through her, a tidal wave of need that drowned all thought and reason. She forgot to think, forgot her own name.

She'd never known it could be like this...

She responded uncertainly at first, then soon gripped his shoulders, clutching him to her.

All her hatred for Santiago, all her earlier misery, transformed to heat as he kissed her in the dark winter night on the edge of the sea, invisible waves crashing noisily against the shore.

She didn't know how long they clung to each other in the cold night, seconds or hours, but when he finally drew away, she knew she'd never be the same. Their breath mingled in the dappled moonlight.

They stared at each other for a split second as scattered snowflakes started to fall.

Wordlessly, he took her hand and pulled her toward the house. She heard the crunch of frozen snow beneath her scuffed black flats, felt the warmth of his hand over hers.

They entered the nineteenth-century mansion, with its dark oak paneling and antique furniture. Inside, it was dark and quiet; it seemed everyone, including the household staff, had gone to bed. Santiago closed the tall, heavy door behind them and punched a code into the security system.

They rushed up the back stairs, hardly able to stop kissing long enough to stumble to the second floor.

Belle shivered. She couldn't be doing this. Impulsively offering her virginity to a man she didn't even like, let alone love?

But as he pulled her into a guest bedroom at the far end of the hall, she couldn't even catch her breath. His long black coat fell to the floor, and he pulled her into his arms. Cupping her face in his hands, he ran his thumbs along her swollen lower lip.

"You're so beautiful," he whispered, running his hands through her long brown hair tangled with ice and snowflakes. "Beautiful, and *mine*…"

Lowering his mouth to hers, he kissed her hungrily. Heat flooded through Belle, making her breasts heavy, swirling low and deep in her core. His hands stroked her deliciously, mesmerizing her with sensation, and by the time she realized he was unzipping her black dress, it was already falling to the floor.

An hour ago, she'd hated him; now she was half-naked in his bedroom.

Setting her back onto his bed, he pulled off his suit jacket, vest and tie. He never took his eyes off her as he unbuttoned his black shirt. His bare chest was chiseled and muscular, curving in the light and shadow. Falling beside her on the bed, he pulled her against him with a growl, kissing her with a hot embrace. He nibbled down her throat, and she tilted her head against the pillow, closing her eyes. He cupped each breast over her white cotton bra and reached beneath the fabric to stroke and thrum the aching nipples beneath.

Unhooking her bra, he tossed it to the floor and lowered his head to suckle one breast, then the other. The sensation was so sharp and wild and new that she gasped, gripping his shoulders tightly.

Moving up, he covered her gasping lips with his own, plundering her mouth before he slowly kissed down her body to her flat, naked belly. His tongue flicked her belly button. Then he kept going down further still.

His hands gripped her hips. He nuzzled between her legs, and she felt the warmth of his breath between her thighs. He held her firmly, gently pressing her legs apart, kissing each of her thighs before he pulled her panties off. Pushing her thighs apart, he teased her with his warm breath, then, with agonizing slowness, he lowered his mouth and tasted her.

The pleasure was so unexpected and explosive that her fingernails dug into his shoulders as his tongue slid against her, hot and wet.

Holding her hips, he worked her with his tongue until

she gripped the blanket beneath her, holding her breath until she started to see stars. He licked her softly one moment, then the next plunged his tongue inside her. She heard a voice cry out, and realized the voice was hers.

He swirled his tongue against her, increasing his rhythm and pressure until her back started arching from the bed. He pushed a single thick finger inside her, then two, stretching her wide. She gasped as the pleasure built almost too high to bear. Higher—higher—then—

Soaring to the sky, she exploded into a million pieces, falling to the earth in gently chiming shards. It was like nothing she'd ever experienced. It was pure joy.

Lifting up from her, he ripped off the last of his clothes. Positioning himself between her legs, he gripped her naked hips. As she was still gasping with pleasure, he pushed his huge, thick shaft inside her.

He'd dreamed of this.

For four months, Santiago had dreamed of seducing the sinfully beautiful woman who'd made it such a point to scorn him. He'd dreamed of having her deliciously full curves in his arms, her body naked beneath his. He'd dreamed of kissing her full pink lips and seeing her lovely face darken with ecstasy. He'd dreamed of taking her, filling her, satiating himself with her.

But now, as he finally pushed inside her, he felt a barrier he had not expected. He froze. He'd never once dreamed of this.

"You're a virgin?" he breathed in shock.

Slowly, she opened her eyes. "Not anymore."

He set his jaw. "Did I hurt you?"

"No," she said in a small voice.

Something in her expression made him tremble. Something in her voice spoke directly to his soul. He felt a strange emotion in his heart: tenderness. He bit out, "You're lying."

"Yes." Her soft, slender arms reached up around his shoulders and pulled him down, down, down against her, tempting him to his own ecstasy and ruin. "But don't stop," she whispered. "Please, Santiago…"

Hearing his name on her lips, he sucked in his breath. How could even a romantic, idealistic woman like Belle Langtry be an untouched innocent, in this modern world? *A virgin.* Santiago was the only man who'd ever touched her, this infuriating, exhilarating, magnificent woman.

His soul felt the danger of getting close to any woman so innocent and bright. It made him want to flee.

But his body, held still deep inside her, felt the opposite as he looked down at her beautiful face, glowing with wanton desire. He shuddered. Ravaging hunger built inside him, thrilling his nerves, coursing down his limbs and centering at his hard core barreled deep inside her.

He lowered his head to hers. His kiss was gentle at first, then deepened, turning to pure light. His hands roamed slowly down her naked body, cupping and caressing her breasts.

She had the most perfect body, curvy and ripe. Any man would die to have a fiery goddess like this in his bed. And that this goddess was also a *virgin*…

He shuddered a little, and without realizing it, pushed deeper inside her. The soft whisper of a moan escaped her as he lowered his lips to suckle her breasts. Her breath changed to a gasp of ecstasy.

Gripping her hips, he very slowly started to ride her, even as he kissed her lips and caressed her breasts. He sucked her earlobe and slowly licked and nibbled down her neck. He felt her body lift beneath his as new pleasure rose in her, and she began to kiss him back hungrily.

He started to lose the last shreds of his self-control. She

was wet, so wet, and somehow her tight sheath accepted all of him. His thrusts became deeper as he wondered if the size of him would be too much for her. But it wasn't. He felt her tighten around him, gripping her fingernails into his shoulders. But that small pain only added to his building pleasure. When he heard her low gasp rise to a scream of joy he could no longer hold back. His eyes closed in pure ecstasy, his head tossing back as he filled her deeply, until his own roar exploded in the deep dark silence of the bedroom. Flying in a whirlwind, he experienced pure sexual joy such as he'd never known before as he spilled himself into her.

He fell back to the bed against her, eyes closed, cradling her body against his own. For ten seconds, as he held her, he felt a deep peace, a sense of home, sweeter than he'd ever known.

Then his eyes flew open. He was filled with regret so great it tasted like ash in his mouth.

"You were right," Belle sighed, a hopeful smile on her lovely heart-shaped face. "I feel recklessly alive. That was like nothing I ever dreamed. Pure magic." She pressed back against his naked chest, pulling his arms more tightly around her, as she said dreamily, "Deep down, maybe you're not all bad. I might even like you a little."

Santiago looked down at her grimly in the moonlight from the bedroom window. He'd just known ecstasy that he'd never experienced before.

With a virgin.

A *romantic*.

Sleeping with Belle had done strange things to him. His body had never known such deep pleasure. And his soul…

She yawned. "I just hope no one heard us."

"They didn't," he said harshly. "Letty and Darius are in the other wing, and this house is made of stone." Stone like his heart, he reminded himself.

"Good. I'd never live it down if Letty knew, after everything I've said about you."

"What did you say to her?"

"I said you were a selfish bastard without a heart."

His shoulders tightened. "I'm not offended. It's true."

"You're funny." She looked up at him sleepily. "You know, no matter what you think, love and marriage aren't always a prison sentence. Look at Letty and Darius."

"They *look* happy," he said grudgingly, then added, "Looks can be deceiving."

Her forehead furrowed. "Don't you believe in anyone? Anything?"

"I believe in myself."

"You're a terrible cynic."

"I see the world as it is, rather than as I wish it could be." Eternal love? A happy family? At thirty-five, Santiago had seen enough of the world to know those kind of miracles were few and far between. Tragedy was the normal state of the world. "Do you already regret sleeping with me?"

Shaking her head, she smiled up at him, looking kittenish and shy and so damned beautiful that his heart caught in his throat. "You feel so good to me. I'm glad you're here." She yawned, closing her eyes, cuddling against him. "I couldn't bear to be alone tonight. You saved me…"

Pressing against his chest, she fell asleep in seconds.

Santiago yearned to sleep, as well. His body wanted to stay like this, with her, cuddled in this warm bed, taking solace in each other against the cold January night and all the other cold nights to come.

Warning lights were flashing everywhere.

He looked down at her, sweetly sleeping in his arms, so soft and beautiful, so opinionated and dreamy and kind. So optimistic.

You saved me.

Santiago felt bone-weary. Carefully, he disentangled

himself from her. Rising from the bed, he walked naked to his coat crumpled on the floor. Pulling his phone from his pocket, he dialed the number of his pilot.

The man struggled not to sound groggy. It was eleven o'clock on a cold winter's night. "Sir?"

"Come get me," he replied. "I'm at Fairholme."

Without waiting for a reply, Santiago hung up. He looked back at Belle one last time, sleeping in his bed, so beautiful in the moonlight. Like an innocent young woman from another time. He couldn't remember ever being that innocent, not with the upbringing he'd had.

Whatever Belle might say, she would want to love him. She would try, like a moth immolating herself against an unfeeling flame.

Of course she would. He was her first.

His jaw tightened. He never would have seduced her if he'd known. He had a rule. No virgins. No innocent hearts. He never brought anyone to his bed who might actually care.

And he'd just seduced an innocent virgin. The friend of Darius's wife.

He felt a low self-hatred. After Nadia, he'd vowed never to get involved with anyone again. Why risk your capital on an investment that was a guaranteed loss? Might as well flush your money—or your soul—straight down the drain.

He thought again of *Wuthering Heights*. He'd never read the book, but he knew it ended badly. It was romance, wasn't it? That always ended badly. Especially in real life.

Santiago silently dressed, then picked up his overnight bag. But he hesitated at the door, still hearing the wistful echo of her voice.

Don't you believe in anyone? Anything?

He'd lied to her. He'd told her he believed in himself. But the real answer was no.

Belle would wake up alone in bed and find him gone.

No note would be needed. She'd get the message. He really was the heartless bastard he claimed to be.

As if there was ever any doubt, he jeered at himself. Regret and self-loathing filled him as he turned down the hall.

He wished he'd never touched her.

CHAPTER TWO

SHIVERING IN THE warm July twilight, Belle stood on the sidewalk of Santiago's elegant residential street on Manhattan's Upper East Side. She watched well-dressed guests step out of glossy chauffeured cars, climbing up the steps and ringing at his door, to be greeted by his butler.

A butler, she thought bitterly. Who had a butler in this day and age?

Santiago Velazquez—that was who.

But the butler wasn't the problem. Belle watched a crowd of beautiful young socialites, giggling and preening, hurry up the steps of his brownstone in six-inch heels and designer cocktail dresses.

She looked down at her own loose, oversized T-shirt, stretchy knit shorts and flip-flops. She wasn't wearing makeup. Her brown hair was pulled back into a messy ponytail. She'd fit in at his fancy party like a dog driving a car.

She didn't belong here. And she didn't want to see Santiago again—*ever*—after the cold way he'd treated her after they'd slept together in January. Losing her virginity in a one-night stand with the heartless, cynical playboy was a mistake she would regret the rest of her life.

But she couldn't leave New York. Not without telling him she was pregnant.

Pregnant. Every time she thought of it, she caught her breath. It was a miracle. She didn't have any other word to describe it, when seven years ago she'd been told very firmly by a doctor that it could never happen. Pregnant.

A dazed smile traced Belle's lips as she rested her hands gently over the wide curve of her belly now. Somehow, in that disastrous night when Santiago had seduced her, this one amazing, impossible thing had happened. She'd gotten her heart's deepest desire: a baby of her own.

There was just one bad thing about it.

Her smile faded. Of all the men on earth to be her unborn baby's father…

She'd tried to tell him; she'd left multiple messages asking him to call her back. He hadn't. She'd been almost glad. It gave her a good excuse to do what she wanted to do—leave New York without telling him he was going to be a father.

But her friend Letty had convinced her to make one last try. "Secrets always come out," she'd pleaded. "Don't make my mistake."

So, against her better judgment, here Belle was, stopping at his luxury brownstone on her way out of town. The last place she wanted to be.

Just thinking of facing Santiago for the first time since he'd snuck out of her bed in the middle of the night, she wanted to turn and run for her pickup truck parked two blocks away, then head south on the turnpike, stomp on the gas and not look back until she reached Texas.

But she'd already made the decision to try one last time to give him the life-changing news that he was going to be a father. Belle always tried to do the right thing, even if it hurt. She wasn't going to turn coward now. Not over *him*.

Tightening her hands into fists, Belle waited until the last limousine departed, then crossed the street in the fading twilight. Her body shook as she walked up the stone steps and knocked on the big oak door.

The butler took one look at her, then started to close the

door as he said scornfully, "Staff and delivery entrance at the back."

Belle blocked the door with her foot. "Excuse me. I need to see Santiago. Please."

The butler looked astonished at her familiar use of his employer's first name, as if a talking rat had just squeaked a request to see the mayor of New York. "Who are you?"

"Tell him Belle Langtry urgently needs to see him." She raised her chin, struggling to hide her pounding heart. "It's an emergency."

With a scowl, the butler opened the door just enough for her to get through. The soles of Belle's flip-flops slapped against the marble floor of the mansion's elegant foyer. She had one brief glimpse of the beautiful, wealthy society crowd in the ballroom, sipping champagne as waiters passed through with silver trays. Then she sucked in her breath as she saw the party's host, head and shoulders above the crowd. With his height and dark good looks, Santiago Velazquez towered over his guests in every way.

The butler pointed down an opposite hallway haughtily. "Wait in there."

Through the door, Belle found a home office with leather-bound books and a big dark wood desk. Knees weak, she sank into the expensive swivel chair. Her cheeks still burned from seeing Santiago from a distance. Thinking of seeing him face to face, she was terrified.

The night he'd taken her virginity, passion and emotion had been like a whirlwind, flinging her up into the sky, to the stars, scattering pieces of her soul like diamonds across the night. It had been so sensual, so spectacular. More than she'd even dreamed it could be.

Right until the moment he'd abandoned her, and she'd had to go down to breakfast alone. She'd had to hide her hurt and bewilderment, and smile at Letty and Darius and their baby, pretending nothing had happened, that nothing was wrong. That was how cold-hearted Santiago was. He'd only promised one night, true. But he hadn't even been able to stick *that* out.

Leaving Fairholme, she'd returned to her tiny apartment in Brooklyn, which she shared with two rude, parent-funded roommates who'd mocked her dreams, her Texas accent—which was barely noticeable!—and her job as a waitress. Normally she would have let their taunts roll off her like water off a duck's back, but after her night with Santiago, she'd felt restless, irritable and hopeless, as she continued to be rejected at auditions, with a day job that barely paid the bills.

A month later, when she'd discovered she was pregnant, everything had changed. Her baby deserved better than this apartment shared with strangers, an insecure future and unpaid bills. Her baby deserved better than a father who couldn't be bothered to return phone calls. It was a bitter thought.

Belle had come to New York with such high hopes. After nearly a decade spent raising her two younger brothers, she'd finally left her small town at twenty-seven, determined to make her dreams come true.

Instead, she'd made a mess of everything.

She'd dreamed of making her fortune? She now had ten dollars less in her wallet than when she'd left Texas eighteen months ago.

She'd dreamed of seeing her name in lights? She'd been rejected from every talent agency in New York.

But worst of all… Belle swallowed hard… She'd dreamed that she would finally find love, real love, the kind that would last forever. Instead, she'd allowed herself to get knocked up by a man she hated.

Belle had had enough of New York. She was going home. Her two suitcases were already packed in her truck, ready to go. There was only one thing left on her to-do list.

Tell Santiago Velazquez he was going to be a father.

But now, she suddenly wasn't sure she could do it. Even seeing him in the ballroom, from a distance, had knocked her for a loop. Maybe this was a mistake. Maybe she shouldn't stay...

Santiago pushed through the door. When he saw her sitting in his chair, his glare was like a blast of heat, his tall, powerful body barely contained by the well-cut suit. "What the hell are you doing here?"

After all these months, this was how he greeted her? She stiffened in the chair, folding her arms over her belly. "Good to see you, too."

Closing the door behind him, Santiago pierced her with his hard, black eyes and said dangerously, "I asked you a question. What are you doing here, Belle? I think I made it very clear that I never wanted to see you again."

"You did."

Santiago moved closer in the shadows of the study. "Why did you trick my butler into letting you in, telling him there was an emergency?"

"It wasn't a trick. It's true."

"An emergency. Really." His lips twisted scornfully. "Let me guess. After all these months, you're realized you can't live without me, and you're here to declare eternal love."

She flinched at the cold derision in his voice.

"God help any woman who truly loved you." She took a deep breath, then glared back at him. "Don't worry. I hate you plenty. More than ever."

A strange expression flashed across his features, then he gave her a cold smile. "Fantastic. So why did you interrupt my party?"

He was glaring at her with such hatred. How could she possibly tell him she was pregnant with his baby? "I came to tell you...I'm leaving New York..."

"That's your emergency?" He gave an incredulous laugh. "One more thing to celebrate today, on top of closing a business deal."

Her hackles rose. "Let me finish!"

"So do it, then." He folded his arms, looking down at her as if he were king of the mountain and she was just a peasant in the dirt. "And let me get back to my guests."

She took a deep breath.

"I'm pregnant."

Her small voice reverberated in the silence of the study. His black eyes widened in almost comical shock.

"What?"

Slowly, she rose from the chair, dropping her arms to her sides so he could see her baby bump beneath her pregnancy-swollen breasts and oversized T-shirt. For a moment, he didn't speak, and she held her breath, afraid to meet his gaze. Some stupid part of her still hoped against hope that he would surprise her. That he would suddenly change back to that warm, irresistible man she'd seen so briefly that cold January night. That he'd gather her into his arms and kiss her joyfully at the news.

Those hopes were quickly dashed.

"*Pregnant*?"

She risked a look at him. His jaw was hard, his eyes dark with rage.

"Yes," she choked out.

She never expected what he did next.

Pulling her close, he put his large, broad hands over her cotton T-shirt, to feel the unmistakable swell of her pregnant belly.

He dropped his hands as if he'd been burned. "You said it was medically impossible."

"I thought it was…"

"You said you could never get pregnant!"

"It's a…a miracle."

"Miracle!" He snorted, then narrowed his eyes. He slowly looked her over. "And here I thought you didn't have what it took to be on Broadway. No gold digger ever lied to my face so convincingly. I actually thought you were some angelic little innocent. Quite the little actress after all."

That low, husky, Spanish-accented voice cut right through her heart, and she staggered back. "You think I got pregnant on purpose?"

He gave a low laugh. "You really had me going with the way you defended true love. Letting me find you alone, sobbing in the garden over the fact that you could never, ever have a baby. I'm impressed. I had no idea you were such an accomplished liar."

"I didn't lie!"

"Cut the act, and get to the part where you give me a price."

"Price?" she said, bewildered.

"There's only one reason you would deliberately trick me into not using a condom when you fluttered your eyes and lured me into bed—"

Her voice came out an enraged squeak. "I never did that!"

"And that's money. But I'll admit," he said carelessly, looking her over, "you earned it. No woman has ever tricked me so thoroughly. Except—" His expression changed, then he set his jaw. "How much do you want?"

"I don't want money." The room was spinning around her. "I just thought you had the right to know!"

"*Perfecto*," he said coolly. Going to the door, he opened it. "You told me. Now get the hell out."

Belle stared at him in shock, astounded that any man could react to news of his unborn son or daughter so coldly, refusing to even show interest, much less take responsibility! "That's it? That's all you have to say?"

"What did you expect?" he drawled. "That I'd fall to one knee and beg you to marry me? Sorry to disappoint you."

Belle stared up at him, incredulous. She'd waited for twenty-eight years, dreaming of Prince Charming, dreaming of true love—and *this* was the man she'd slept with!

Anger rose like bile in her throat. "Wow. You figured me out. Yes, I'm desperate to marry you, Santiago. Who wouldn't want to be the bride of the nastiest, most cold-hearted man on earth? And raise a baby with you?" She gave a harsh laugh. "What an amazing father you would make!"

His expression hardened. "Belle—"

"You call me a liar. A gold digger. When you know I was a virgin the night you seduced me!" She lifted her chin, trembling with emotion. "Was this what you meant when you called me naïve? Did you decide you wanted to be the one to show me the truth about the heartless world?"

"Look—"

"I never should have come here." Tears were burning the backs of her eyes. But she'd let him see her cry once, that dark January night, and he'd lured her into destruction with his sweet kisses and honeyed words. She'd die before she let him ever see her weak again. "Forget about the baby. Forget I even exist." Stopping at the door, she looked back at him one last time. "I wish any man but you could have been the father of my baby," she choked out. "It's a mistake I'll regret the rest of my life."

Turning, she left, rushing past the snooty butler and beautiful, rich guests who looked like they'd never had a single problem in their glamorous lives. She went outside, nearly tripping down the steps into the cooling night air. She ran halfway down the block in her flip-flops before she realized Santiago wasn't following her.

Good. She didn't care. When she reached her old 1978 Chevy pickup, she started up the engine with a roar. Her hands didn't stop shaking until she was past the Lincoln Tunnel.

From the first day they'd met, she'd known Santiago was dark-hearted poison. How could she have been so stupid to let him seduce her?

For one night, let me give you joy. Without strings. Without consequences.

Belle choked out a sob as she gripped the steering wheel, driving south on the Jersey Turnpike. She was thrilled about the baby, but what she would have given to have any other man as the father!

For the last few months, when Santiago hadn't returned her phone messages, she'd told herself that she and the baby would be better off without him. But part of her had secretly hoped for another miracle—that if she told Santiago she was pregnant, he'd want to be a father. A husband. That they could all love each other, and be happy.

So stupid.

She wiped her eyes. Instead Santiago had not only cavalierly abandoned his unborn baby, he'd insulted Belle and thrown her out of his house for daring to tell him she was pregnant!

The truly shocking thing was that she was even surprised. He'd made his feelings clear from the beginning. He thought babies were a thankless responsibility and love was for suckers.

Belle cried until her eyes burned, then at midnight, pulled over to a roadside motel to sleep fitfully till dawn.

The next day, the hypnotic road started to calm her. She started feeling like she'd dodged a bullet. She didn't need a cold, heartless man wrecking her peace of mind and breaking their child's heart. Better that Santiago abandon them now rather than later.

By the third day, as the mile markers passed and she left the green rolling hills of east Texas behind, she started to recognize the familiar landscape of home, and her heart grew lighter. There was something soothing about the wide horizons stretching out forever, with nothing but sagebrush and the merciless summer sun in the unrelenting blue sky.

Feeling a sweet flutter inside her, Belle put a hand to her belly. "So be it," she whispered aloud. This baby would be hers alone. She would spend the rest of her life appreciating this miracle, devoting herself to her child.

It was still morning, but already growing hot. The air conditioning in her pickup didn't work, but both windows were rolled down, so it was all right. Though she was lucky it wasn't raining because one of them wouldn't roll back up.

As she drew in to the edges of her small town, she took a deep breath. *Home.* Though it wasn't the same, without her younger brothers. Ray now lived in Atlanta and twenty-one-year-old Joe in Denver. But at least here, the world made sense.

But as she pulled into the dirt driveway, she abruptly slammed on the brake.

A big black helicopter was parked in the sagebrush prairie, tucked behind her house.

She sucked in her breath. A helicopter? Then she saw the two hulking bodyguards prowling nearby. That could only mean…

With an intake of breath, she looked straight at the old wooden house with the peeling paint. Her heart stopped.

Standing on the wooden porch, with arms grimly folded, was Santiago.

What was he doing here?

Fear pounded through her as she turned off the engine of her truck.

With a deep breath, Belle got out of her old pickup, tossing her long brown ponytail, slamming the door with a rusty squeak.

"What are you doing in Texas?" She lifted her chin to

hide the tremble in her voice. "Let me guess. Did you think up some new ways to insult me?"

He came down the rickety wooden steps toward her, his black eyes glittering. "Three nights ago, you showed up at my house with a very shocking accusation."

"You mean I accused you of getting me pregnant?" Waving her arm, she said furiously, "Such a horrible accusation! No wonder you wanted me to get the hell out!"

Standing on the last step above her, he ground his teeth. "I was calling your bluff. It was a negotiation. I expected you to swiftly return with a demand for a specific sum of money."

Calling her announcement of pregnancy a negotiation! He was just the worst! A lump rose in her throat. Blinking fast, she turned toward his entourage and helicopter in the field. She said evenly, "How did you find my address?"

"Easy."

"You must have been waiting for hours."

"Twenty minutes."

"Twenty! How?" She gasped. "There was no way you could know when I'd get here. Even I didn't know exactly!"

He gave a grim smile. "That was more difficult."

"Were you tracking my truck? Spying on me?"

"Stop changing the subject," he said coldly. He stepped closer on the packed dirt driveway, towering a foot over her. His black eyes traced the length of her body, from her oversized T-shirt to her shorts to her flip-flops, and a flash of heat coursed through her. "You were telling the truth? The baby is mine?"

"Of course the baby's yours!"

"How can I trust a proven liar?"

"When did I lie?" she said indignantly.

"'I can't get pregnant, ever,'" he mimicked. "'It's impossible.'"

"You are such a jerk." Belle shivered, sweating beneath the hot Texas sun.

His voice had been low, controlled, but she felt his cold fury. He was all gorgeous on the outside, she thought, like melted chocolate with his soulful Spanish eyes and black hair and hard-muscled body. Too bad his soul was even harder than his body. He had a soul like flint. Like ice.

Just when she'd been counting her blessings that he was out of their lives, here he was, pushing back in. For what purpose?

"You made your choice," she whispered. "You abandoned us. This baby is mine now. Mine alone."

He lifted a dark eyebrow. "That's not how paternity works."

"It is if I say it is."

"Then why tell me you were pregnant at all?"

"Because three days ago I was foolish enough to hope you could change. Now I know it would be better for my baby to have no father at all than a man like you." She lifted her chin. "Now get off my land."

Growing dangerously still, Santiago stared at her, jaw tight. Without a word, he turned to stare across the stark horizon against the wide blue sky. Against her will, her eyes traced the golden glow of the sun gleaming against his olive-colored skin, the chiseled cheekbones, the dark scruff on his jaw.

"Let me tell you what's going to happen, Belle." When he looked back at her, his voice was low and deep, almost a purr. "Today, you're going to get a paternity test."

"What? Forget it!"

"And if it's proven that the baby's mine," his black eyes glittered, "you're going to marry me."

Was he crazy or was she?

"*Marry* you?" Belle gasped. "Are you out of your mind? I hate you!"

"You should be pleased. Your plan worked. Admit you purposefully got pregnant with my child to trap me into marriage. Have that much respect for me, at least."

"I won't, because it's not true!"

"I'll admit I made a mistake, trusting you. I should have known better. I should have known your innocence was a lie. I shall pay for that." He moved closer with a gleam in his dark eyes. "But so will you."

A shiver went through her.

"I would never marry someone I hate," she whispered.

"You're acting like you have a choice. You don't." He gave a cold smile. "You'll do what I say. And if the baby is mine…then so are you."

CHAPTER THREE

Santiago Velazquez had learned the hard way that there were two types of people in the world: delusional dreamers who hid from the harsh truth of the world, and those clear-eyed few who could face it, and fight for what they wanted.

Belle Langtry was a dreamer. He'd known that the day they'd met, at their friends' wedding last September, when she'd chirped annoyingly about the bridal couple's "eternal love" in face of their obvious misery. Belle's rose-colored glasses were so thick she was blind.

But then, you'd have to be blind to see anything hopeful about love or marriage. Love was a lie, and any marriage based on it would be a disaster from start to finish. It could only end in tears. He should know. His mother had been married five times, to every man in Spain except Santiago's actual father.

But for some reason, when he'd met Belle, so feisty and sure of her own illusions, he hadn't been irritated. He'd been charmed. Petite, curvaceous, dark-haired, with deep sultry eyes and a body clearly made for sin, she'd gotten under his skin from the beginning. And not just because of her beauty.

Belle hated him, and wasn't afraid to show it. With one glaringly big exception, Santiago couldn't remember any woman scorning him so thoroughly. Not since he'd grown into his full height at twenty, and especially not since he'd made his fortune. Women were always hoping to get into his bed, his wallet, or usually both. He hadn't realized just how boring it had all become until that exact moment that Belle Langtry had insulted him to his face.

She was different from the others. She drew him like a flame in the darkness. Her tart tongue, her apparent innocence, her brazen honesty, had made him lower his defenses. Their single night together had been transcendent and joyful and raw. It had almost made him question his cynical view of the world.

Then, three nights ago, he'd discovered how wrong he'd been about her.

Belle Langtry wasn't different. She wasn't innocent. She'd only pretended to wear rose-colored glasses to hide the fact that she was a cold-eyed liar, just like everyone else, plotting for her personal gain. She wasn't like his mother had been, pathetically desperate for love, deceiving herself to the end of her self-destructive life. No. Belle was like Nadia. A mercenary gold digger who would say or do anything, her eyes always on the glittering prize.

At Fairholme, in the snowy garden that cold January night, when Belle had wept in Santiago's arms as if her heart was breaking, she'd been *lying*.

When he'd softly stroked her long dark hair in the moonlight and whispered that everything would be all right, and Belle had looked up, her big dark eyes anguished beneath trembling lashes, she'd been *lying*.

When she'd told him she could never, ever get pregnant, and lowering his head, he'd kissed her beneath the moonlight scattered with snowflakes, as he tried to distract her from her grief, she'd been *lying*.

Santiago had known Belle was an actress. He'd just had no idea how good. He hadn't been fooled in such a way in a long time.

After she'd invaded his cocktail party and dropped the bomb of her pregnancy news, he'd paced and snarled at his guests, wondering what he'd do when Belle finally returned to make her financial demands. If she was truly pregnant with his child, she had leverage. Because as much as Santiago despised the idea of love and marriage, he would never abandon a child the way he himself had once been doubly abandoned.

What would Belle ask for? he'd wondered. Marriage? A trust fund in the baby's name? Or would she eliminate the middleman and simply ask for a billion-dollar check, written out directly to her?

He'd waited that night, nerves thrumming, but she'd never returned to his town house. The next morning, he'd discovered she'd left New York, just as she'd claimed she intended.

Now, after three days, he knew everything about Belle, except for her medical records, which he expected to have later today. His investigator had easily found her home address in Texas. The GPS of her phone had been tracked through means he didn't care to know, and someone had watched for her highly visible blue 1978 Chevy at the gas station two hours to the east, the only gas station for miles in this empty Texas prairie. He'd simply taken the helicopter here from his large ranch in south Texas.

But he could hardly be expected to reveal his strategies to an enemy. Which was what Belle now was.

From the day they'd met, she'd acted like she hated him. But he'd never hated her.

Until now.

Santiago stared down at her beneath the unrelenting furnace of the sun blasting heat from the Texas sky. He felt a prickling of sweat on his forehead. Wearing a vest, tie and long-sleeved shirt along with tailored wool trousers, he found the temperature brutal. And it wasn't even noon.

Santiago set his jaw. He wouldn't allow Belle to control the situation. Or his baby. He didn't know her goal, but the way she was playing the game—like a professional poker player without a heart—the amount she wanted must be astronomical. And why would it ever stop, when she'd have the leverage to control him for the rest of her life? She could try to control custody, or make their child hate him through her lies. She could leave Santiago like a fish gasping on a hook.

Belle had deliberately misled him, saying she couldn't get pregnant. Later, she'd ambushed him with her news and then fled New York, just to show him she meant business. She'd done all this for a reason. To get the upper hand.

But he wouldn't let her use their innocent baby as a pawn. He couldn't be forced or tricked into abandoning a child. Not after what he'd endured himself as a boy. Belle didn't know who she was dealing with. Santiago would scorch the earth to win this war.

His eyes narrowed. She thought she could defeat him? He'd fought his way from an orphanage in Madrid, stowing away at eighteen on a ship to New York City with the equivalent of five hundred dollars in his pocket. Now, he was a billionaire, the majority owner of an international conglomerate that sold everything from running shoes to snack foods on six continents. You didn't do that by being weak, or letting anyone else win.

Belle was in his world now. His world. His rules.

"I'll never marry you," she ground out, her brown eyes shooting sparks. "I'll never belong to you."

"You already do, Belle," he said flatly. "You just don't know it yet." Turning, he made a quick gesture to his helicopter pilot, who started the engine.

She gave an incredulous laugh over the rising noise of the helicopter. "You're crazy!"

Santiago looked down at her. Even now, despising Belle as his enemy, he felt more drawn than ever. She wasn't conventionally beautiful, perhaps, but somehow she was more seductive than any woman he'd ever known. His eyes unwillingly traced the curve of her cheek. The slope of her graceful neck. The fullness of her pregnancy-swollen breasts.

Belle was right, he thought grimly. He was crazy. Because even knowing her for a lying, almost sociopathic gold digger, he wanted her in his bed more than ever.

"I'd be crazy to abandon my child to you," he said evenly. He looked over his shoulder at the wooden house in the barren sagebrush field, with only a few wan, spindly trees overlooking a dry creek bed. "Or to this."

Following his gaze, she looked outraged. "You're judging me because I don't live in a palace?"

"I'm judging what you've done to escape it," he said grimly. He knew all about how she'd been raised here, and only left a year and a half before. He wondered if her dream of Broadway stardom had always been a cover story, and she'd planned to hook a rich man from the beginning. Maybe even her friendship with Letty had been contrived, to better throw Belle in the path of wealthy targets.

The only thing good about this isolated, bare land was the view of the endless blue sky. The sky above the dry grass prairie was starkly dramatic. You could see forever. The freedom. The unending loneliness.

But there were all kinds of loneliness. You could be lonely surrounded by others, as he'd learned as a child.

His own son or daughter would never know that kind of loneliness. He or she would never feel unwanted, or alone. He would see to that.

He turned away. "Let's go."

"Where?"

"Paternity test."

"Forget it—"

He whirled on her with narrowed eyes. "You hate me," he growled. "Fine. I feel the same for you. But does not our child, at least, deserve to know the truth about his parents?"

She glared at him, her eyes glittering with dislike. Then her expression faltered. He'd found the one argument that could sway her.

"Fine," she bit out.

"You'll take the test?"

"For my baby's sake. Not yours."

He exhaled. He hadn't realized he'd been holding his breath, wondering if he'd have to physically force her into the helicopter—a very unpleasant thought, especially with a woman who was likely pregnant with his child. He was relieved she wasn't being so unreasonable.

Then he realized Belle must have decided to change her strategy. She was just shifting her ground, like a boxer. Santiago's lips pressed together in a thin line. He glanced at his bodyguards, hovering nearby. "Get her things."

As his men reached into her pickup, Santiago took her arm, leading her forward. Within seconds, she was sitting comfortably beside him on a leather seat inside the luxury helicopter.

"I'll take the test, but I'm never going to marry you," she said over the sound of the propellers.

He narrowed his eyes coldly. "We both know this is exactly what you wanted to happen. So stop the act. In your heart, I know you are rejoicing."

"I'm not!"

"Your joy will not last long." He drew closer, his face inches from hers. "You will find that being my wife is different than you imagined. You won't own me, Belle. I will own you."

Her brown eyes got big, and he felt a current of electricity course through his body. Against his will, his gaze fell to her lips. So delicious. So sensual and red. Heat surged through his veins.

He'd always despised the idea of marriage, but for the first time, he saw the benefits. As much as he hated her, it had only lifted his desire to a fever. And he knew, by the nervous flicker of her tongue against her lips even now, that Belle felt the same.

Once wed, she would be in his bed, at his command, for as long as he desired. Because one thing, at least, hadn't been a lie between them.

So why wait?

For all these months, since the explosive night he'd taken her virginity, he'd denied himself the pleasure of her. Both for his own sake and, he'd once believed, for hers.

No longer.

Tonight, he thought hungrily. He would have her in his bed tonight.

But first things first.

Putting on a headset, Santiago spoke to the pilot over the rising noise of the blades whipping the sky. "Let's go."

Sitting in the helicopter, Belle looked through the window across the wide plains of Texas. Far below, she saw wild horses running across the prairie, feral and free, a hundred miles away from any human civilization.

She envied them right now.

"Those are mine." Santiago's voice came through her headset. Sitting on the white leather seat beside her, he nodded toward the horses with satisfaction. "We're on the north edge of my property."

So even the wild horses weren't free, she thought glumly. It was the first time they'd spoken in the noisy helicopter since they'd left the world-class medical clinic in Houston.

"You want to own everything, don't you?"

"I do own everything." Santiago's dark eyes gleamed at her. "My ranch is nearly half a million acres."

"Half a—" She sucked in her breath, then said slowly, "Wait. Did you buy the Alford Ranch?"

He raised a sardonic eyebrow. "You've heard of it?"

"Of course I've heard of it," she snapped. "It's famous. There was a scandal a few years ago when it was sold to some foreigner—you?"

He shrugged. "All of this land was once owned by Spaniards, so some people might say that the Alfords were the foreigners. I was merely reacquiring it."

She looked at him skeptically. "Spaniards owned this?"

"Most of South Texas was once claimed by the Spanish Empire, in the time of the conquistadors."

"How do you know that?"

He gave a grim smile. "My father's family is very proud of their history. When I was a boy, and still cared, I read about my ancestors. The family line goes back six hundred years."

"The Velazquez family can be traced six hundred years?" she blurted out. She barely knew the full names of her own great-grandparents.

"Velazquez is my mother's name. My father is a Zoya. The eighth Duque de Sangovia."

His voice was so flat she wasn't sure she'd heard him right. "Your father is a duke? An actual duke?"

He shrugged. "So?"

"What's he like?" she breathed. She'd never met royalty before, or aristocracy. The closest she'd come was knowing a kid called Earl back in middle school.

"I wouldn't know," he said shortly. "We've never met. Look." Changing the subject, Santiago pointed out the window. "There's the house."

Belle looked, and gasped.

The horizon was wide and flat, stretching in every direction, but after miles of dry, sparse sagebrush, the landscape had turned green. Between tree-covered rivers, she saw outbuildings and barns and pens. And at the most beautiful spot, she was astonished to see a blue lake, sparkling in the late afternoon sun. Next to it, atop a small hill surrounded by trees, was a sprawling single-story ranch house that made the place in the old TV show *Dallas* look like a fishing shack.

"It's beautiful," she said in awe. "The land is so green!"

"Five different rivers cross the property."

Past one of the pens she saw a private hangar, with a helipad and airplane runway stretching out to the horizon beyond. "All this is yours?"

"All mine."

His black eyes gleamed down at her, and she heard the echo of his arrogant words earlier. *If the baby is mine, then so are you.* She shivered.

The baby was his. He now had undeniable proof. When they'd gone to the cutting-edge medical clinic in Houston, she'd gotten the impression Santiago must be a very important financial donor, the way the entire staff had waited on him hand and foot. They'd taken the noninvasive blood test, drawing blood from each of them, then the highly trained lab technicians had promised to rush the results.

"But while you wait—" the female OB/GYN had smiled between them "—would you like to have an ultrasound, and find out if you're having a boy or girl?"

Belle had started to refuse. She'd already decided she wanted to be surprised at the birth. But looking at Santiago's face—his dark eyes so bright, almost boyishly eager as he looked at her—she couldn't refuse. If Santiago truly wanted to be what she herself had never had...a loving father...then she was going to do everything she could to encourage the bond between father and child.

"All right," she'd said quietly, and got up on the hospital bed. A few minutes later, as the doctor ran the wand over the sticky goo on her belly, they were staring at the image on the ultrasound screen. A *whoosh-whoosh* sound filled the room.

"What's that?" Santiago asked in alarm, sitting beside her on the bed.

Belle blinked at him in surprise. She suddenly realized that unlike her, he was hearing that sound for the very first time. Smiling, she told him, "It's the baby's heartbeat."

"Heartbeat?" he breathed. The expression on his darkly handsome face, normally hard and cynical, changed so much he looked like a different man.

"It's nice and strong. Your baby looks healthy," the doctor murmured. She pointed at the ultrasound screen. "Here you can see the head, arms…legs…and…" She turned to them with a smile. "Congratulations. You're having a little girl."

"A girl!" Belle gasped.

"A girl?" Reaching out, Santiago suddenly gripped Belle's hand tightly in his own. "When will she be born?"

"Her growth is on track for her due date in late September," the doctor replied.

"September," he murmured, looking dazed. "Just two months from now…"

Belle saw an expression on his face she'd never seen before. Bewilderment. Emotion. Tenderness.

So he wasn't a total bastard after all, she thought. There was one thing that could reach past his layers of cynicism and darkness. Their baby.

Grateful tears had risen unbidden to her eyes, and she'd gripped his hand back tightly. Their daughter would have a father. A father who loved her.

Now, as the helicopter landed at his Texas ranch, Santiago held out his hand to help her out onto the tarmac. He caught her when her knees unexpectedly started to buckle.

"Are you all right?" he asked, his eyes full of concern.

She gave him a weak smile. "It's been a crazy week."

He laughed. "That's one way of describing it."

She'd never seen him laugh like that, with his whole body, almost a guffaw. It made him more human, and somehow even more handsome, more impossibly desirable. In that instant, as she looked up at his dark, merry eyes, her heart twisted in her chest. She turned away, afraid of what he might see in her face.

"So, what happens now?" she said, relieved her voice held steady.

"Now?" he said. "We start planning the wedding."

She stopped abruptly on the tarmac. "I'm not going to marry you. We can share custody."

His eyes narrowed. "The decision has been made."

"By you. Not by me. And if you think you can bully me into marriage, on this ranch or anywhere else, you've got another think coming." She lifted her chin. "My family might not have an aristocratic history that goes back to infinity, but there are a few things we do have."

"Enlighten me."

"Stubbornness. Pure cussedness. And I'm not going to marry a man I don't love, a man who doesn't love me. I would rather scrub your floors with my tongue!"

Amusement flashed across his handsome face. "That can be arranged. Although," he murmured in her ear, "I can think of better uses for your tongue."

An unwilling fire went through Belle's body. Before she could formulate a response, he took her hand, pulling her toward the sprawling single-story ranch house surrounded by green trees.

Inside the main house, it was light and airy, with large windows and hardwood floors. A smiling housekeeper came forward. "Welcome back to the ranch, Mr. Velazquez." She turned her rosy round face in Belle's direction. "Welcome, miss. I hope you had a nice journey."

Nice didn't quite cover it, but luckily Santiago answered

for her. "It's been a long day, Mrs. Carlson. Could you please serve refreshments in the morning room?"

"Of course, Mr. Velazquez."

He led Belle down the hall, into a large room with a glossy wooden floor and a wall of windows. Comfortable furniture faced the view of green trees and a river turned gold beneath dappled sunlight. She breathed, "It's so beautiful."

"Sit down," he said. He seemed suddenly on edge.

Her knees felt weak anyway, so she let herself fall back onto the soft, plush, white cotton sofa. A moment later, the housekeeper appeared with a tray, which she set down on the table.

"Thank you."

"Of course, sir."

After the housekeeper departed, Santiago handed Belle what looked like a cocktail from the tray. At her dubious look, he explained, "Sweet tea."

Oh, her favorite. She practically snatched it from him. Drinking deeply, she sighed in pleasure at the ice-cold, sweetened, nonalcoholic beverage. Wiping her mouth, she sank back happily into the cushions of the sofa. "There are a few things about you that aren't horrible."

"Like sweet tea?"

"You're not totally a monster."

"You're welcome."

Gulping down the rest of the drink, she held the empty glass out hopefully.

His lips quirked as he turned back to the tray. Refilling her glass with the ceramic pitcher, he poured one for himself. "By the way, if you're formulating a plot to run away, you should know the nearest highway is thirty miles."

"I'm not planning to run away."

He straightened. "You're not?"

"Why would I? You're my baby's father. We have to figure it out. For her sake."

He stared at her. His handsome face seemed tense. He held out a plate. "Cookie?"

"Thank you." Chocolate chip, warm from the oven. As she bit into it, the butter and sugar and chocolate were like a burst on her tongue. She sighed with pleasure, then, feeling his gaze on her, looked up, pretending to scowl. "If you're trying to ply me with delicious food and drink to convince me to marry you, it won't work. However," she added hopefully, "you're free to keep trying."

But he just looked at her, his handsome face strained. He started to say something, then abruptly changed his mind. "Excuse me, I have to go."

"Go? Go where?"

"I'll have Mrs. Carlson show you the bedroom. As you said," he gave a smile that didn't reach his eyes, "it's been a crazy week. Rest, if you like. I'll see you for dinner. Eight o'clock."

He left without another word.

Now what was that all about? Although she wasn't going to complain, since at least he'd left the tray. Taking another cookie from the plate, Belle looked out at the leafy green trees moving softly in an unseen breeze, dappled with golden afternoon light. He'd gone to all that trouble to drag her to his ranch, and now, instead of threatening her into marriage or trying to boss her around, he'd just fed her sweet tea and home-baked cookies, then left her to relax?

But then, people had continually surprised her in life, starting with her own family. Belle couldn't remember her father, who'd died when she was a baby. She'd grown up in that house on the edge of the sagebrush prairie with a stepfather, two younger half brothers and her sad-eyed mother, who tried unsuccessfully to shield her children from both her sorrow and her terminal illness. Belle's stepfather, a wiry, laconic welder, never showed much interest in any of the children. He worked long hours then spent his evenings smoking cigarettes, drinking his nightly six-pack and yelling at his wife.

But when Belle was twelve, her mother died, and everything changed. Her stepfather started yelling at her instead, threatening to kick her out of the house, "Because you're none of mine."

So she'd anxiously tried to earn her keep by taking care of the young boys, by cooking and cleaning. By always being cheerful and smiling. By making sure she was never any trouble to anyone.

A week after Belle graduated from high school, her stepfather died suddenly of a brain aneurysm. Ray was thirteen, Joe just eleven. There were no other relatives, no life insurance and almost no savings. Rather than let her little brothers be turned over to foster care, Belle gave up a college scholarship to stay in Bluebell and work as a waitress to support them, raising them until they were grown.

It hadn't been easy. As teenagers, her orphaned brothers had gotten into fights at school, and Ray had briefly gotten into drugs. Those years had been filled with slammed doors, yells of "I hate you!" and her homemade dinners thrown to the floor.

Barely more than a teenager herself, Belle had struggled to get through it. Heartsick, exhausted and alone, she'd dreamed about falling in love with a man who was handsome and kind. A man who would take care of her.

Then, at twenty-one, she had. And it had nearly destroyed her.

"Miss Langtry?" The plump, gray-haired housekeeper appeared in the doorway with her ever-present smile. "If you're done, I can show you to your room."

Glancing at the empty tray, Belle said dryly, "I guess I'm done."

Pushing herself up from the sofa—a simple act that was getting harder by the day as her belly expanded—she followed the housekeeper down the hall of the ranch house. They turned down another hallway, then Mrs. Carlson pushed open a door. "Here's your bedroom, miss."

The room was enormous, with a tall ceiling, a walk-in closet and an en suite bathroom. This, too, had a wall of windows overlooking the river. But that wasn't the bedroom's most notable characteristic.

Belle stared at the enormous bed.

"Is something wrong, Miss Langtry?"

"Um…" Looking around the enormous bedroom, Belle managed, "This is a really nice guest room."

Her worst fears were realized when the older woman replied with a laugh, "Guest room? I know they say everything's bigger in Texas, but honey, that would be crazy. This bedroom suite is bigger than most houses. It's the master bedroom."

Belle gulped. But before she could think of a good reply to explain there was *no way* she was going to be sleeping with the master in this bedroom, the housekeeper continued to the bathroom, proudly showing off the marble tub, sparkling silver fixtures and fresh flowers, with a skylight overhead. Now this, Belle could appreciate.

"You'll find everything you could need or want… Mr. Velazquez said you were weary and dusty after traveling. We have everything you need for a nice, long bath."

She showed Belle all the perfumes, French soaps, creams, shampoos so expensive that she'd only read about them in celebrity magazines. Belle had always thought rich people must be fools for spending fifty dollars on shampoo when the cheap generic brand got your hair just as clean. But as she sniffed the expensive shampoo tentatively, it did smell nice.

"Mr. Velazquez trusts you'll be comfortable while he

conducts some business this afternoon." She opened a door. Belle followed her into a huge closet, with a chandelier and a white sofa.

The housekeeper indicated a red dress hanging alone in the closet. "He requests that you wear this tonight. Dinner will be served on the terrace at eight."

Looking at the dress, Belle breathed, "It's beautiful."

"There are shoes to match, two-inch heels so you won't be uncomfortable or off balance." She smiled in the direction of Belle's belly. "And also new lingerie." She opened one of the drawers. "Silk. Here. Next to your other things."

Lingerie? Belle blushed, suddenly unable to meet the other woman's eyes. Looking around the huge closet, she saw a few scant clothes that had already been unpacked from her suitcase. But other than that and the red dress, the enormous walk-in closet's racks and shelves were empty. "Where are Santiago's clothes?"

"Mr. Velazquez's clothes are in the master closet."

"Isn't this the master closet?"

"Oh, no." Her friendly, chubby face widened in a broad smile. "This closet is designated just for the mistress of the house, that is, if there ever should be one." Leaning forward, she confided, "You're the first woman he's ever brought to the ranch."

"I am?"

"Goodness. Getting late." Mrs. Carlson looked at her watch. "Everything you'll need is here. We arranged toiletries, lotions, lipsticks, everything we could think of that you might want. My grandson is in a school play down at Alford Elementary tonight. The rest of the staff will be gone by eight."

"You all don't live here?"

"Oh, goodness, no. There are staff cottages on the other side of the lake. You and Mr. Velazquez can be completely alone." Was it her imagination, or did the housekeeper wink? "Good night, miss."

Belle stared indignantly after her. Why had she winked? What did she think would happen if she and Santiago were alone?

Nothing, she thought firmly, and locked the bedroom door to prove it. She glanced at the enormous bed. As comfortable as it looked, she would never share it with Santiago. But since he wasn't here right now...

She climbed onto the soft, comfortable bed as days of worry and weariness caught up with her. Her head hit the pillow and she closed her eyes just for a moment.

When she woke, she realized by the fading sunlight that she'd accidentally slept for hours.

Rising from the bed, Belle saw the red dress hanging in the walk-in closet across the bedroom. Going to it, she let her fingertips stroke the soft fabric. She saw the designer tag and gulped. She didn't know fashion, but even she had heard of that famous designer. And the shoes!

But it would be bad manners not to wear it. Especially since it was the most beautiful thing she'd ever seen in real life, much less worn on her body.

Taking the dress and silk lingerie, she went to the enormous en suite bathroom and took a shower. As she stepped naked beneath the hot, steaming water, with six different spigots coming at her from all sides, she sighed in pleasure as the dust and heartbreak of the last three days were swept away. She tried the shampoo. Maybe the fifty dollars was worth it, she thought in a blissful haze. Though even a bargain shampoo would have been great in a shower like this.

Wrapping herself in a towel, she brushed out her long, wet hair. Opening a drawer, she found boxes of brand-new makeup, the high-end kind from department stores with the nice packaging, all lined up for her use, next to a variety of brand-new perfumes and pricey scented lotions.

She tried it all, then put on the silk bra and panties. She almost moaned. So sensual. So soft.

Finally, she pulled on the red knit dress, which fit perfectly over her swollen breasts and baby bump. The soft fabric felt like heaven against her perfumed skin. Even her hands, which for the last year and a half had always been red and chapped from working as a waitress at the diner, felt soft, from all the lotions. She looked in the bathroom mirror.

Her hair now gleamed, tumbling down her shoulders, dark against her creamy caramel skin. Her cheeks were flushed pink from the heat of the shower. Her lips were ruby red to match the dress. Her brown eyes gleamed in the shadows beneath dark kohl and mascara.

Even to her own eyes, she looked…different.

Was it this place? The dress? The extravagant shampoo?

Or was it being around Santiago, being pregnant with his child, being the first woman he'd ever brought to this famous ranch, spread across five counties of south Texas?

"Most of South Texas was once claimed by the Spanish Empire, in the time of the conquistadors…my father is a Zoya. The eighth Duque de Sangovia."

Santiago, the son of a duke? That surprised her. He didn't seem like a man who'd been born with a silver spoon in his mouth. Oh, he was arrogant enough. But he seemed too rough, like a man who'd had to fight so hard for everything that he no longer gave a damn about the judgment of lesser mortals.

"Your father is a duke? An actual duke?… What's he like?"

"I wouldn't know. We've never met."

That was one thing Santiago and Belle had in common, then. All she had of her father was an old picture of him, beaming into the camera as he held her as a swaddled baby, sleeping in his arms.

If Santiago had never even met his father, that explained a lot. But why did they have different last names? If his father was still alive, why had the two men never met?

Then she was distracted by a more urgent question. Biting her lip, Belle looked down at her belly, prominent in the red dress. She looked at the dress, at the luxurious toiletries, the costly, well-made shoes.

Why was Santiago suddenly being so kind to her?

She couldn't trust it, that was for sure. She'd learned that from their night together. He could be warm and tender when he wanted her, then ruthlessly toss her out of his life like garbage.

There could be only one reason. He'd realized he couldn't bully her into marriage, so he was going to try to seduce her into it.

She wouldn't let him.

She *wouldn't*.

Belle was willing to share custody of their baby. But she wouldn't share her life, her heart and certainly not her body. She would never be Santiago Velazquez's plaything again, and definitely not his wife.

Now she just had to convince him of that, so he'd let her go home.

At five minutes past eight, as Belle walked through the enormous, sprawling ranch house, down the darkened hallways, she felt strangely nervous of how he'd react.

Opening the sliding doors, she went outside onto the terrace that stretched out toward the lake. Fairy lights hung from a large pergola, covered with flowers of pink bougainvillea. The lights twinkled against the twilight as soft music came from invisible speakers.

And she saw him.

Santiago stood at the terrace railing, looking out pensively toward dark water painted red by sunset. Then he turned, devastatingly handsome, tall and broad-shouldered in his tuxedo. And he smiled.

"Welcome," he said in his low, husky voice. Their eyes locked, and held.

And Belle suddenly knew the real reason for her fear. Her heart had known it all along, and so had her body. Her brain had refused to accept it. Now she saw the truth. She hadn't been afraid of Santiago's reaction.

She was afraid of her own. Because when she'd given him her body all those months ago, she'd unwillingly given him part of her heart. And now, as he smiled at her, his eyes twinkling beneath the lights, she caught her breath.

"You're beautiful." Coming closer, he held out a champagne glass. His dark eyes caressed her as he whispered, "Brighter than the stars."

As she took the champagne glass, their fingers brushed. She saw the intention in his eyes, and it rocked her to her core.

Santiago intended to conquer her, just as he'd conquered the world. He intended to win her, as he'd won his billion-dollar fortune. He intended to rule her, as he ruled this isolated Texas ranch, big enough to be its own kingdom.

He intended to possess her as his wife. And he would not be denied.

CHAPTER FOUR

HE'D BEEN WRONG about her. All wrong.

When he'd left New York in pursuit of Belle, he'd been certain she was a gold digger, a cunning, cold-hearted actress, who'd ruthlessly lied in order to conceive his child for her own selfish financial gain.

But that afternoon, at the medical center in Houston, he'd learned otherwise.

Standing in the hallway outside the examination room as he waited for Belle, he'd stared at the doctor in disbelief. "Is this a joke?"

She'd smiled. "I never joke about medical matters."

"What do you mean, she was telling the truth?"

"Miss Langtry had good reason to think she could never conceive a child," the doctor had said. "I just received her medical records from the hospital in Bluebell. Seven years ago, she had a procedure to make pregnancy impossible. Bilateral tubal ligation." She hesitated. "I shouldn't be discussing this with you, but…"

But she was, and they both knew why. Santiago spent many millions of dollars each year supporting her clinic, so uninsured patients could get world-class care without worrying about payment. He still remembered his first winter in New York, at eighteen, when he'd been sick for months but hadn't gone to a doctor because he'd feared the cost.

Now, he said incredulously, "Belle deliberately had surgery to make sure she'd never get pregnant? Why?"

"You'd have to ask her."

"But she was only twenty-one—and a virgin! What crackpot doctor would perform such a procedure?"

"Interestingly, that doctor retired a month later. It turned out he'd been suffering from the early stages of dementia."

"So if she had that surgery seven years ago, how can she be pregnant?" Santiago said.

The doctor hesitated. "Miss Langtry is young…"

"So?"

"There is a risk of healing after that type of procedure. It's rare, but it does happen. The body finds a way. It's even more likely when the patient is young."

Santiago glared at her. "She honestly believed she couldn't get pregnant."

"Yes. Either the procedure wasn't done correctly, or her body healed over the last seven years."

It had been like a punch in the gut.

Everything Santiago had believed about Belle was wrong. She wasn't a greedy climber. She was innocent. She'd been telling the truth all along.

After they left the medical center, as their helicopter flew south from Houston, Belle had refused to meet his gaze, but he hadn't been able to look away from her. Her beautiful face, her lush body, pregnant with his child. Remembering their night together, he'd felt aware of her every movement. He'd thought of nothing but how she'd felt in his arms that night. How she'd gasped with ecstasy. How afterward, she'd cuddled against him so sweetly.

"You feel so good to me," she'd whispered. *"I'm glad you're here. I couldn't bear to be alone tonight. You saved me…"*

Santiago had left her that night because he'd known his life would change, with her in it. And he hadn't wanted it to change.

But his life had changed without his consent. In spite of incredible odds, she was pregnant.

Now there was someone else to think about. His child. Having his paternity confirmed, seeing his daughter pictured on the ultrasound screen in Houston, the idea of a baby had felt truly real to him for the first time. A daughter. An innocent child. She hadn't asked to be conceived, but now it was possible, through no fault of her own, she could be born without a name. Without a father's protection or love.

He couldn't let that happen.

He couldn't let his child be split between parents, and have the same childhood he'd endured, ignored and rejected by his biological father, watching his mother so desperate to be loved that she married man after man, each less worthy than the last.

No. His daughter's life would be different.

She would have a stable home. Married parents. Financial security. His daughter would have a happy childhood, filled with love.

When they'd arrived at the ranch that afternoon, Santiago had already made up his mind. He'd taken Belle straight to the morning room, intending to force an engagement ring on her hand, to blackmail or threaten her into it, if he had to. But something stopped him.

The thought of their daughter.

After the way he'd treated Belle from the moment they'd slept together that cold winter's night, she'd had good reason to despise him. He'd abandoned her. Ignored her phone messages. Treated her badly when she'd actually come to his house to tell him about the baby.

Standing in the morning room, he'd known he could force Belle to marry him, if he chose.

He suddenly didn't want to.

He didn't want to be her enemy. For their daughter's

sake, they needed a better foundation for their marriage, for a happy home, than resentment and hatred.

So Santiago had abruptly changed tactics.

Instead of giving Belle his ultimatum in the morning room, he'd given her time to rest, to regroup, to be refreshed. And he'd taken time to plan his own strategy. He'd organized this dinner with the help of his staff. The dress had already been purchased in nearby Alford, by Mrs. Carlson, but he'd still lacked one thing: a show-stopping engagement ring.

Fortunately, he'd thought with grim amusement, he happened to have one, gathering dust these past years in his safe. The diamond ring was tucked in his tuxedo pocket now, glinting, sparkling, obscene.

He'd tried to give this ring to a different woman, long ago; one he'd loved so much he'd built his billion-dollar fortune in the attempt to win her. Santiago still felt acid in his gut at the memory of the day he'd proposed to Nadia with this very ring, as promised so many years before, only to discover she hadn't waited for him. And the man she'd chosen—

Santiago's shoulders went tight. In the past. All in the past. Starting today, he would treat Belle, the mother of his unborn child, with respect and care. Once he did, she would see reason. She would not refuse his marriage proposal.

The sun was falling into the lake, a red ball of fire burning through the low haze of twilight, when Santiago heard Belle come out through the sliding doors onto the terrace. Turning from the railing, he looked at her.

And was dazzled.

He'd never seen such rampant beauty, all lush curves in that red dress, her dark hair tumbling over her shoulders, her lips invitingly red, black eyelashes trembling over big brown eyes.

"You're beautiful," he breathed, holding out a champagne glass. "Brighter than the stars."

She took the glass. From this close, her skin looked delectably soft. He wanted to kiss her. He wanted to pick her up like a caveman and carry her to bed, to rip off the red dress that clung to every curve, and make love to her until he felt her quiver and shake, until he heard her cry out with pleasure.

She looked up at him, her eyes regretful. "I can't drink champagne."

"It's sparkling juice."

"Juice?" Taking the glass, she gave him a nervous smile. "I can't imagine you drinking anything except black coffee and maybe Scotch."

"We're celebrating."

"We are?"

"And if you can't drink champagne, neither will I."

Her forehead furrowed in the twilight, beneath the fairy lights of the pergola.

"I think I know why you're being so nice to me," she said slowly.

"Because I know I was wrong," he said quietly. "And I'm sorry."

She could have no idea, he thought, how long it had been since he'd said those last two words to anyone. Years? Decades?

"Sorry?" She frowned. "About what?"

"You truly thought you couldn't get pregnant."

Her expression changed. "Why do you believe me now?"

"Dr. Hill told me about your medical procedure."

"She shouldn't have." She stiffened. "That's my private business."

"Not anymore. Anything that relates to you or the baby is my business now." Moving closer, his body thrummed with awareness as his gaze fell to her red lips, then further down still. Her thick dark hair fell in waves over her bare clavicle, over her shoulders, almost to her full breasts straining the red knit fabric of her dress. His body suddenly raged to pull her into his arms, tip her back against the table and ravage her right here and now. He took a deep breath to control himself.

"Won't you join me?"

Turning toward a large stone table nearby, he showed her the dishes, interspersed with big vases of flowers.

"What is it?" she said doubtfully.

"Dinner." He lifted a silver lid off the largest platter. Frowning, she peeked over his shoulder. When she saw the food, she burst into a full-bodied, incredulous laugh that he felt down to his toes.

"Blueberries? Licorice whips? I thought you'd try to serve me something nasty, like caviar!"

"I have only your favorites." He lifted another silver lid, and grinned as he heard her gasp.

"Ham and pineapple pizza!" she exclaimed. "Are you kidding me?"

"With the ranch and hot sauce you like, for dipping," he said smugly. "And for dessert…" He opened a third silver lid to reveal strawberry shortcake, thick sweet cakes covered with plump, juicy strawberries and thick dollops of whipped cream. Now, she looked at him almost in awe.

"How did you know?" she breathed.

"Magic."

"No, seriously."

"I called Letty and asked her what you liked best." He lifted an eyebrow. "She didn't sound particularly shocked to hear from me, by the way."

Her cheeks colored. "She's the only one I told about you. I knew she wouldn't tell anyone you were my baby's father.

Not after what she went through with Darius." Tentatively, she touched the crust. "The pizza is still hot!"

"I told you." He waved a hand airily. "Magic."

She looked at him skeptically.

He rolled his eyes. "There's a hot plate beneath the tray. If you make me explain, it takes the magic away. All that's left is cheap tricks." He started to add, *just like romance*, but stopped himself, since he didn't think it would help his cause. Pulling out a chair, he gave her a sensual smile. "Have a seat."

As they ate together, enjoying fruit, pizza, sparkling water and finally dessert, the sun gradually disappeared beneath the horizon, turning the sky a soft pink against the black lake.

He enjoyed watching her eat. He took pleasure in her appetite. As she started her third piece of strawberry short-cake, he leaned forward and brushed his fingertips against the corner of her mouth.

"Missed some whipped cream," he said, and then licked it off his fingertips. Belle's eyes went wide, and he heard her intake of breath. He almost kissed her then. Instead, he leaned back in his chair to look at her.

"So why did you do it, Belle?" he asked quietly. "Why did you deliberately have surgery at twenty-one, to prevent pregnancy? Knowing you as I do, it doesn't make sense."

For a moment he thought she might not answer. Then she set down her spoon.

"My dad died when I was a baby," she said haltingly. "My mother remarried a few years later, and had my brothers…"

"I know."

Belle looked surprised. "You know?" She glanced down as his hand enfolded her own, then said with a tinge of bitterness, "Of course you know. Your private investigator told you, right?" She gave a humorless laugh. "So you know my mother died when I was twelve and my stepfather six years later. I couldn't let my brothers be sent to foster care. So I gave up my dream of college and stayed home to raise them."

Santiago tried to think of a time he'd made a sacrifice that big for anyone. He couldn't.

"It wasn't easy," she continued in a low voice. "They were angry teenagers. Sometimes I wasn't sure I could make it. Then I met Justin." She blinked fast. "He was so strong and sure. He said he loved me. Even when I told him I was old-fashioned and wished to wait until marriage to have sex, he still wanted me…"

Santiago gave an incredulous laugh. "No sex until marriage?"

"I know." She smiled wistfully. "Crazy, right? But he'd just gotten divorced. His wife'd had an awful miscarriage that broke them up. Justin was ten years older than me, but he said that didn't matter. He was even willing to help me raise my brothers, who desperately needed a male role model."

"Did they?" he said evenly, remembering all the times his own mother had married so-called "male role models" who hadn't been worth much and hadn't lasted more than a year.

"It seemed like the perfect solution for everyone to be happy. There was just one catch." Her voice was small. "Justin couldn't go through losing a baby again. So he only agreed to marry me if I…he and I…made sure to never have a baby of our own. Ever." She looked down at her lap. "So a few weeks before our wedding, I did it. It seemed like the only way to make everyone happy."

"What about you? Did it make you happy?"

A strangled laugh escaped her lips, and she looked away. "Not exactly."

The final light of the setting sun streaked across her pale, troubled face. He said grimly, "What happened?"

"He left me. Right before our wedding." She gave him a small smile. "He'd had a hard time waiting for sex and ran into his ex-wife at a bar. One thing led to another, and she became pregnant. After that, he wanted to give their relationship another try. He told me he'd never stopped loving her."

He gave a low, heartfelt curse in Spanish.

"It's all right," she said quietly. "They're happy now. They're married, living in El Paso. Last I heard, they have a big rambling house and five children."

Santiago fell silent, his jaw tight.

"I know what you're thinking." She looked up, her eyes suddenly shining with unshed tears. "Go ahead. Tell me how stupid I was, to sacrifice my own dreams for the sake of love."

Rising moonlight frosted the dark lake, and he heard the plaintive call of unseen birds. He looked at her beauty, at the way her dark eyelashes trembled against her cheeks.

Rising to his feet, he took her hand. "Dance with me."

"No, I…"

"Why?" He gave her a wicked smile. "Are you afraid?"

"Of course not. I'm just not a good dancer, I…"

But he didn't listen to her excuses. Gently, he pulled her from the chair, into his arms. He felt her body tremble against his. The fairy lights twinkled above the terrace, as they looked out at the moon-swept lake. They were alone.

"I'll lead," he murmured, and he twirled her slowly around the flagstone terrace. He watched her sway, light as air. Saw the beauty of her. The kindness. The way she'd sacrificed for her younger brothers. The way she'd sacrificed for the man she'd once thought she would marry.

Damn, he thought. What a mother she will make.

What a *wife*.

He whirled her close, then caught her tight in his arms. Her eyes widened, and she sucked in her breath as she saw his intention.

Slowly, never taking his eyes from hers, he lowered his mouth to hers.

She didn't fight him, but closed her eyes, letting him hold her close. He closed his eyes and kissed her, really kissed her.

Lightning shattered through his body, through his soul, in the embrace. He felt her tremble, pressing her body against his.

Then she ripped away, her eyes tortured.

"Why are you doing this?" she choked out.

"Doing what?"

"*Romancing* me," she said bitterly, "like the night you seduced me. I'm not going to fall for it again, so you can break my heart!" She pressed her palm against his chest, pushing him away. "Just tell me what you want from me."

The stars above them sparkled in the wide, velvety black sky as he looked down at her. It was too soon. He had barely started to seduce her as he wished. But she wanted him to speak plainly, so he would. He had that much respect for her.

"Very well," he said quietly. Reaching into his tuxedo jacket pocket, he lowered himself to one knee, holding up the huge diamond ring. It glittered brighter and bigger than the full moon shining across the endless Texas sky. "I want you to marry me, Belle."

She gaped at him, looking from the ring to his face and back again.

"I know I've treated you badly," he said. "But I'll never make that mistake again. I'll lie to you, Belle. We'll be more than lovers. We'll be partners. Parents. I know you want love, and I regret I cannot give you that. But I offer you something better."

"Better than love?" she whispered. He nodded.

"My loyalty. You never betrayed me. I will never betray you. I've made very few promises in life, but I'm making one to you now. If you marry me, I'll make sure you're never alone again. Our marriage will be for life."

"For life?" She looked stricken. She said hoarsely, "I might consider a temporary marriage…to give our baby a name…"

"No." His expression hardened. "A real marriage, Belle. A real home. Isn't that what you want? Isn't that what our baby deserves from us?"

She looked away and whispered, "I don't know."

Rising to his feet, he pulled her close and growled, "I think you do."

Her dark gaze seared his. "I want to marry someone I can love and respect. And you're not that man, Santiago, you know you're not."

The words caused a stab in his solar plexus. He hadn't known he could still be hurt by rejection. He'd thought he'd buried his heart long ago. To be hurt now, when he was trying his best to please her, when he was trying his best to be honest, stung him to the core.

He took a deep breath. "Love—perhaps not. But we both love our daughter. And if you give me a chance," he said in a low voice, "I will earn your respect. I swear it."

She looked at the fairy lights and the flowers on the stone table, at the diamond ring still in his hand.

"I'm not your toy," she said in a small voice. "Just because we slept together once and conceived this child, you can't just have me whenever you want amusement. You don't have any permanent claim over me."

"You're wrong." He lifted his gaze to hers. "I do have a permanent claim. Just as you've had a claim over me, from the moment you came to my bed."

"What are you talking about?"

"You," he whispered, cupping her cheek. "And how you've bewitched me."

Her eyes were big as she looked up at him. "You can find someone else—"

"*No.*"

"Yes you can! You've been with dozens of women since that night. Supermodels, actresses, socialites…" Her voice cut off as their eyes met. She choked out, "Haven't you?"

Never looking away, he shook his head, his jaw tight. "There's been no one. Because I don't want any other woman. I haven't, since our night together. I've only hungered for you." He narrowed his eyes as he looked down at her. His voice was a growl. "You will belong to me, Belle. You have no choice. I already belong to you."

I already belong to you.

It wasn't romantic. At all. He said it, Belle thought, as if he felt trapped. Oppressed, even. His dark eyes glittered.

"Are you telling me," she breathed, "you've been celibate all these months?"

"Yes." His voice was a low growl.

"But—but why?"

His eyes were dark. "You've ensorcelled me."

Ensorcelled. Such a strange, old-fashioned word. Such a gleam in his dark eyes and his powerful body towering over her with all his strength. She suddenly felt like she'd gone back hundreds of years, to a simpler time.

Belle shivered, struggling not to feel so aware of his body close to hers. His eyes were dark beneath the softly swaying lights. She saw the arrogant curve of his dangerously seductive mouth.

He was right, she realized. She did belong to him. From the moment he'd kissed her that cold January night.

No. She couldn't pretend it had been just that. It had been more.

She'd been able to be honest with him that night in a way she hadn't been since her mother died. She never had to pretend with Santiago. She didn't have to act cheerful and happy all the time. She could actually be herself.

She did want him. His warmth. His strength. She wanted the man who'd seduced her that cold winter's night, not just with his body, but with his words.

The only thing that kept her from falling into his arms now was remembering how she'd felt waking up alone that gray January morning, and all the mornings after, when he ignored message after frantic message.

"But I can't trust you," she said in a small voice. "Not anymore. If I give myself to you, how do I know I won't be left broken-hearted and alone?"

"Your heart will be safe. I'll never ask for it." Reaching out, he stroked her shoulder. His soft touch over the fabric of her red dress felt like fire. "And you'll never be alone again." He lifted her hand to his mouth. She felt the warmth of his breath as he kissed her palm, then the back of her hand. "Never," he whispered.

She couldn't hide her shiver beneath his seductive caress. Looking up at his darkly handsome face beneath the moonlight, at his powerful body towering over hers in the tuxedo, she wondered wildly if he could hear the pounding of her heart. "I can't…"

"Are you sure?" he whispered. Brushing back her hair, he kissed her forehead. Her cheeks. She trembled in his arms, hovering on the edge of surrender.

"Please don't do this." Pressing her palms against the lapels of his tuxedo jacket, she lifted her tearful gaze to his. "You don't know what you're asking me."

"So tell me."

Her hands tightened.

"To give up all hope of being loved," she choked out. "Now and forever."

"That kind of love is an illusion." He drew back. "I know. My mother was a maid working in my father's palace when she got pregnant with me. He was already married, and his duchess was heavily pregnant. He must not have found his wife sexually appealing, because one afternoon he pushed my mother into a closet and kissed her." His lips twisted. "She was barely nineteen, and so wrapped up in fairy-tale dreams she convinced herself the duke loved her. That only lasted until she got pregnant, too, and he threw her out of the palace. She was suddenly poor, a single mother, and dreams don't pay the bills. She thought only love could save her. So she married. Five times."

Santiago had never told her anything about his childhood before. Not one word. She sucked in her breath. "Five marriages?"

"And each husband worse than the last. Each time, her heart was broken. She didn't want to raise me alone," he said lightly. "She couldn't relax at night. Couldn't sleep. So she took sleeping pills. One night she took too many and died."

"How old were you?" she said, aghast.

"Fourteen. I called an ambulance when I found her. The authorities dragged me from the house and I was sent to an orphanage."

"Why didn't you go to your father?"

He snorted. "My father already had a son and heir. He did not care to recognize the bastard result of his affair with a maid. When I tried to see him at his palace in Madrid, he set the dogs on me."

"How could he?" Belle breathed.

Santiago turned away, blankly staring toward the pearlescent moonlight trailing across the lake. He finally looked at her.

"The man did me a favor," he said flatly. "And I'm doing you one now by telling you this. The fairy-tale dream doesn't exist. Only when you give it up will you have any possibility of happiness."

Belle could understand why he might think that, after everything he'd gone through. And yet... She bit her lip. "You never tried to speak to your father again? Or your half brother?"

"They had their chance." His eyes were hard. "I might have Zoya blood, but they mean nothing to me now."

Santiago looked down at her. "So now do you understand? I never intended this to happen. I never meant to marry, or have a child. What do I know of being a husband, or a father?" His eyes narrowed. "But I will not allow my child to have the lonely existence I had. She will not be rejected, raised in poverty by a delusional mother and a succession of uncaring stepfathers. She will have my name." He looked at her evenly. "You will marry me."

Belle licked her lips as she tried desperately, "But there are other ways besides marriage..."

Reaching out, he cupped her cheek.

"You will agree to marry me, Belle, or I will keep you here until the baby is born, and take the child from you. Do you understand?"

His tone was so gentle, it took her a moment to understand the meaning. Then her eyes went wide as she drew away sharply.

"You wouldn't."

"You are mistaken if you believe I am as soft-hearted as you. I am not."

She shivered, not doubting it. "So you're threatening me?"

"I am telling you how it will be. I won't let you put your own foolish dreams above the needs of our baby. Either you leave here with this ring on your finger, or you don't leave at all."

"You can't want to be married... To be loyal and faithful to one woman for the rest of your life? You don't even love me!"

"I will keep my vows," he said impatiently. "I expect you to keep them as well."

She blinked fast. "It's easy for you to give up all dreams of love. You've never loved anyone."

Her harsh words echoed in the silent evening. He stared at her for a long moment, his jaw clenching. When he finally spoke, his voice held no expression.

"So you agree?"

"Fine," she choked out.

"You accept my proposal?"

"You've left me no choice."

"As you've left me none." He slid the enormous platinum-set diamond over her finger. "This ring symbolizes how we are bound. For life."

The precious metal felt cold and heavy, both on her hand and on her heart. "Now what, a shotgun wedding at the nearest justice of the peace?"

He snorted, then sobered. "We will be married in New York."

Back to New York, the city that had chewed her up and spat her out, with a man who would never love her, and who for all his fine words, was practically blackmailing her into marriage? "This gets better and better."

"Our wedding will be a society event. As my wife, you will take your rightful place in New York society."

Belle looked at him incredulously. "Have you lost your mind? Me? A leader in New York society?"

"You will be."

Belle lifted her chin. "I told you. You don't own me."

Santiago looked down at her, his black eyes glittering. "You're wrong," he said softly. Taking her hand in his own, he looked down at the sharp shine of the ring in the moonlight. "From this moment on, I do."

She felt his hand enfolding hers, his palm rough and warm against her skin, and a skitter of electricity went up her spine. Her lips parted.

He pulled her into his arms, cupping her face in his hands. Deliberately, slowly, he lowered his mouth to hers.

The smooth caress of his hot satin lips seared her, making her weak. Ruthlessly, he deepened the kiss, tilting back her head, tangling his hands in her hair. Need raced through her, quickening her heartbeat, making her lose her breath.

Pressing her against the thick white column of the pergola, amid the bloom of pink flowers beneath the fairy lights, he slowly kissed down her throat. Her head fell back, her dark hair tumbling down, as her eyes closed against the sweet pleasure of sensation.

He ran his hands down her arms, over the soft red knit fabric of her low-cut dress. She felt his touch like a whisper over her full breasts, over her belly, over her hips. He lowered his head to kiss her naked collarbone, then the bare cleavage between her breasts.

"I want you," he whispered. Leaning forward, he whispered against the sensitive flesh of her earlobe, making her shiver, "Come to my bed tonight."

Belle opened her eyes. Frosted by moonlight and the silvery lake behind him, Santiago's face was in shadow as he towered over her like a dark angel. That had been the Spanish playboy's nickname in New York, she remembered. Ángel. Now she understood why.

And she could no longer resist. She could only surrender.

Santiago looked at her, then scooped her wordlessly into his arms. He carried her into the sprawling ranch house, down the silent hallway, into the enormous master bedroom, dark with shadows except for the shaft of moonlight pooling through the large windows.

He set her down almost reverently, and she stood in front of him, unsteady on her feet. Kneeling in front of her, he pulled off her shoes, one by one. Rising, he stood in front of her and kissed her again, deeply. When the kiss ended, as she tried to catch her breath, he circled her, his fingertips lingering against her body, and slowly unzipped her dress in the back. Gently, he drew the dress down her body, slipping it off her full breasts, down her arms. He tugged it slowly over her belly, to her hips, until the dress finally fell like a soft whisper to the floor.

She stood nearly naked in front of him, wearing only a silk bra and panties. Still fully dressed in his tuxedo, Santiago looked down at her in the moonlight.

"So beautiful," he whispered, reaching out to touch her shoulder. His hand traced down to cup a full breast over the sensuous silk bra. She nearly gasped as she felt the warmth of his hand pressing the smooth fabric against her heavy breast and aching nipple, which hardened beneath his touch.

He drew closer. His palms explored the full curve of her belly, down to her hips, stroking the naked skin along the edge of her silk panties. Reaching around her, he put his hands over her backside, taking her firmly in his grasp, pulling her hard against his body.

When he lowered his mouth to hers, his kiss was hungry, as he reached beneath the flimsy silk to cup her naked breasts. His thumb stroked her aching nipple. As she gasped with pleasure, he unclasped the sliver of silk and dropped it entirely to the floor.

He cupped both her breasts with his hands, as if marveling at their weight, then lowered his mouth to gently suckle her.

The sensation was so intense she jolted beneath his hot mouth, gripping his shoulders. Pleasure was rising so hard and fast inside her, she wondered if she could climax like this, with only his lips against her breast, his tongue swirling around her nipple, sucking her deeply into his hot, wet mouth.

She gasped, her fingernails digging into his shoulders. She realized with shock that he was still wearing his jacket. Reaching down, she undid his tuxedo tie, then roughly yanked his jacket down from his shoulders.

Rising, he looked down at her intently. Gaze locked with hers, he undid the buttons of his shirt and trousers then dropped them to the floor, along with his silk boxers. He stood naked, his body hard and jutting toward her. She looked down at him in amazement. Reaching out, she took his hard shaft fully in her hands—it took both her hands—and relished the soft, velvety feel of him, so thick and hard as steel.

Now he was the one to gasp.

With a low growl, he pulled her toward the king-sized bed bathed in moonlight, and drew her on top of him. She was shy and uncertain at first, until he pulled her head down into a kiss. Her dark hair tumbled down like a veil, blocking the moonlight, leaving their faces in darkness.

She felt his hands on her hips, moving her until her legs spread wide over his. She felt the hardness of him, insistent between her thighs, demanding entry. That single movement, feeling him pressing against the wet, aching center of her desire, was enough to make her hold her breath. Involuntarily, she swayed against him. With an intake of breath, he tightened his hands on her hips, lifting her off his body, positioning her. Then, with agonizing slowness, he lowered her again, filling her, inch by delicious inch.

She gasped from the pleasure as he slid inside her. Just when she thought her body couldn't take any more of him, he somehow went even deeper, all the way to the hilt, all the way to the heart.

He was hard and thick inside her as his large hands

gripped her backside, spreading her wide. She gasped, tossing back her head.

Then slowly, instinctively, she began to move her body against his, feeling the deliciously exquisite tension rise and build inside her as she slid against his flat, muscular belly. She felt his rough fingertips gripping into her hips as she began to ride him, harder, faster. Her breasts bounced against the swell of her belly as she rode him, soft and slow, then hard and deep. She rode him until her whole body started to tremble and shake.

As she cried out, she heard his low roar join hers, rising to a shout as he filled her so deep she exploded with joyful ecstasy. Her cry became a scream she didn't even try to contain, and he screamed with her, his body jerking and pulsing as he spilled himself inside her.

Exhausted, she collapsed beside him, and he held her. He cuddled her close, gently kissing her sweaty temple. But as she closed her eyes, she heard his dark whisper, so soft she wondered if she'd imagined it, like a whisper of her heart's deepest fear.

"You're mine now."

CHAPTER FIVE

THE LIGHTS OF New York City were dazzling and bright, but in the deep canyon between skyscrapers, Belle could no longer see the sky.

Sitting beside Santiago in the chauffeured black Escalade, with bodyguards following in another SUV, she'd felt numb as they traveled from the airport in New Jersey through Midtown, passing within blocks of the Broadway and Off-Broadway theaters that had rejected her so thoroughly.

As the saying went, if you could make it in New York, you could make it anywhere. But Belle hadn't made it here. She'd thought if she could be an actress, if she could earn a living by pretending to be someone else every day, she could be happy. Instead, the city had laughed in her face.

And Santiago expected her, a small-town girl who'd never gone to college, to know how to be a socialite in this wealthy, ruthless city?

All she'd ever done was work as a waitress and raise her brothers. If Santiago had needed her to remember six different dinner orders with special instructions and sauce on the side, and serve it all at once balanced on her arms, no problem. If he'd wanted her to rustle up a double platter of brownies for ten hungry teenage basketball players in no time flat, Belle could have handled it.

But knowing how to blend into high society? Knowing how to swan around being chic while making small talk to the highly educated and fashionable glitterati he mingled with?

It was all Belle could do not to hyperventilate.

She glanced mutinously at Santiago sitting beside her in the SUV. "I'm not going to do it."

He didn't even bother to look up from his phone. They'd been having this same argument since before they'd left his Texas ranch that afternoon. "You will."

"I'd only embarrass you. I don't know how to talk to rich people!"

This time, Santiago did look up. His dark eyes flashed with amusement. "You talk to them like people."

She sat back sulkily against the soft black calfskin leather of the luxury SUV. "You know what I mean."

"They're not people?"

"Not *normal* people. They all have advanced degrees from places like Oxford and Princeton. They're billionaire entrepreneurs and ambassadors and famous artists. They all grew up in castles with a full staff of servants…"

"You really are a romantic, aren't you?"

"The point is, we have nothing in common."

"You do." His dark eyes gleamed. "Me."

She stared at him, stricken. Then she turned away, looking out silently at the dark, sparkling city.

Last night, Santiago had brought her to the heights of ecstasy in bed. But he'd also proven how thoroughly he commanded her body, even when her heart tried to resist.

He'd given her deep pleasure, made her feel things— *do* things—she'd never imagined. But that morning, she'd once again woken up alone. Only now, she had a big diamond ring on her left hand.

She'd surrendered to his marriage demand, both for their child's sake and because he'd left her no choice. She'd given up any hope of love. She looked at her engagement ring, glinting beneath the city lights. So hard. So cold.

Like the man who'd given it to her.

Alone in the ranch's master bedroom that morning, she'd gotten dressed in an old stretchy T-shirt from high school, the faded words *Bluebell Bears* emblazoned over the picture of a bear that stretched over her big belly, and a pair of loose khaki shorts and flip-flops. She'd found him sitting at the breakfast table drinking coffee, wearing a sleek black button-up shirt and black pants, more sophisticated than she'd ever be. She'd trembled in the doorway, still feeling last night's kisses, wondering how he would greet her now they were engaged to be married for the rest of their lives.

"Good morning," he'd said, barely looking at her. "I trust you slept well. We will be returning to New York today."

That had been it. No warmth. No friendliness. No acknowledgement of the night they'd spent in each other's arms. No matter how exhilarating, amazing, explosive the lovemaking, it was empty, with no love to fuel the fire.

And now he'd dragged her back to the fairy-tale city that had broken her heart.

Belle whispered in the back of the SUV, "I can't possibly be your hostess in New York society."

"What are you afraid of?"

"They'll laugh in my face. Society people are even meaner than casting directors. I saw what they did to Letty, ripping her apart just because her father went to jail…"

"That was different."

"They're meaner than rattlesnakes." Belle looked down, feeling a lump in her throat as she stared down at the gorgeous, obscenely huge diamond engagement ring. "And they'll all think the same as you did. That I'm a gold digger who tricked you into marrying me, by deliberately getting knocked up."

"No one will think that," he said firmly, and his arrogant expression made her roll her eyes. Santiago really thought he could control everything, even the thoughts of strangers. She shook her head.

"You're just not the kind of man who marries a girl like me. And this ring…"

"What about it?" he said shortly. He sounded on edge. She wondered if she'd offended him.

"It's beautiful, but it looks weird on my hand. I've spent my life working. This ring should belong to a princess who's never had to lift a finger." She looked down at her casual shorts and high school T-shirt over her baby bump. "Your trophy wife should be an heiress or supermodel or movie star or something. Not a short, dumpy waitress."

"Don't talk about yourself like that." His jaw tightened, and his dark eyes turned hard in a way she didn't understand. "And movie stars are highly overrated."

Belle frowned, looking up at his handsome face. "Did you ever date one?"

He blinked, then abruptly turned away, looking at the bright city lights sliding past their chauffeured SUV.

"Romantic love is a dream of lust and lies," he said in a low voice. "It all turns to ash in the end." He turned to her. "Be grateful it's not part of our relationship."

Belle started to protest, then remembered how she'd felt when Justin dumped her right before their wedding. How she'd felt when she'd found out he was not only getting back with his ex-wife, but they were also expecting the baby she could no longer conceive. Love hadn't felt so great back then.

"It's not always like that," she tried.

His cruel, sensual lips twisted. "Give me an example of a romance working out."

"Um…" She tried to think, then said triumphantly, "Letty and Darius."

"That just proves my point. They didn't marry for love.

They got lucky. Or else they decided to make the best of things."

She bit her lip and said in a small voice, "Maybe we can do that, too."

He rewarded her with a smile. "My executive assistant has already planned a meeting with the most exclusive wedding planner in the city."

"You will meet with this planner?"

"No, you will. You're the bride. I have a company to run."

"I didn't realize you were so old-fashioned, with the gender roles."

He flashed a grin. "I know my place. The wedding day always belongs to the bride."

The dread in Belle's stomach only intensified. "I don't need a big wedding. We could just go to City Hall…"

"Like Letty and Darius?"

That shut her up. Though Letty and Darius were happy now, their wedding had been awful, no matter how Belle had tried to put a positive spin on it. "Fine," she said in a small voice. "Have it your way."

Reaching out, he touched her shoulder. "At least we know what we're getting into. Our marriage will last. No delusions of hearts and flowers. You won't expect me to fulfill your every girlish fantasy."

Pulling away, she tossed her head. "You couldn't, even if you tried."

Santiago gave her a sideways glance, his eyes suddenly dark as he murmured, "I could fulfill a few." As she shivered at the huskiness of his voice, the SUV stopped.

"We're here, sir."

"Thank you, Ivan. Come." He turned to Belle. "The staff is waiting to meet you."

"By staff, do you mean that butler I met?" she said nervously.

"Yes, but Jones isn't the only one. We have three live-in staff members. Four others live out."

"Just for you?" she said in dismay. He smiled.

"For us."

The door was opened by their driver, Ivan. As he and Kip, a bodyguard who had tattoos on his neck and a mean stare, brought in their luggage, Santiago helped Belle out of the SUV. Looking up at his brownstone mansion, she gulped.

When she'd first come here a few days ago to tell Santiago she was pregnant, she never could have imagined she'd return as his fiancée and mistress of the house!

Inside the front door, seven uniformed members of staff stood waiting in the enormous foyer beneath the skylight. At the head of the line was the butler who'd been so cold to her when she'd last visited the house. Looking at her, the man narrowed his eyes in a scowl.

Nervously, she tried to draw back, but Santiago held her hand securely.

"Good evening to you all," he said gravely. "Thank you for waiting for our arrival." He glanced at Belle. "I'm pleased to introduce you to my future bride, Miss Belle Langtry."

"Hello, miss."

"Welcome."

"Lovely to meet you, miss."

As each staff member introduced themselves to Belle in turn, she felt embarrassed. She felt like a fraud. Like she belonged in the staff line herself. What did she know about being the lady of the manor? Her friend Letty had been born to it, but Belle didn't have a clue, and she was sure it showed. She ducked her head bashfully.

"As my wife," Santiago continued, "Belle will be in charge of the house, so please teach her everything she needs to know." He glanced at the butler. "I'm relying on you, Jones."

"Of course, sir," the butler intoned, but the sideways glance he threw Belle was far from friendly. *I'm sure we'll be friends in no time*, she told herself, but she felt more ill at ease than ever.

"That's all for now. You may go," Santiago said. After the staff departed, he looked down at her and said softly, "I'll show you around your new home."

He drew her down the hallway of the mansion. The ceilings were high, with molded plaster and chandeliers. Their footsteps echoed on the hardwood and marble floors, walking past walls with oak paneling and stone fireplaces. "How old is this house?"

"Not very. It was built in 1899."

"That's older than my whole hometown," she replied in awe. "And three employees actually live here? Doesn't that feel weird, having your butler around when you're slacking on the sofa in sweatpants, eating chips and watching football on TV?"

He gave a brief smile. "The staff have their own quarters in the evenings. On the fifth floor."

"The *fifth*? How many floors are there?"

"Seven, if you include the basement."

"This isn't a house, it's a skyscraper!"

His smile spread to a grin. "Come on."

Belle's eyes got bigger as he showed her the rest of the house, from the wine cellar and home theater in the basement, to the ballroom—"but it's small, for a ballroom"—on the main floor, through five guest bedrooms and nine bathrooms.

"Why so many bathrooms?" she said curiously. "Is it so when one gets dirty, you don't need to bother cleaning it, but can just move on to the next one?"

He gave her a crooked half grin. "That's not necessary.

The staff takes good care of us. Let me show you my second favorite place in this house."

He led her onto the elevator, causing Belle to exclaim in wonder, "You have your own elevator?", and pressed the button for the roof. As she walked out into the warm, humid July night, she gasped.

A rooftop pool was illuminated bright blue, with lounge chairs and cabanas surrounded by flowers and plants. But the real star was the view. As they stood on the rooftop, fifty-floor skyscrapers surrounded them, shining brightly.

Going to the edge of the railing, Belle saw, far below, the noise and traffic of the street. There was only one dark spot, directly to the left: Central Park.

"Wow," she breathed, then looked at Santiago. "If this is only your second favorite part of the house, what's your first?"

His eyes were dark, his voice low. "I'll show you."

He led her back to the elevator, and pressed the button for the third floor, which she realized she hadn't seen at all yet. The elevator door opened on a small foyer. Beyond that was a single door.

"What's this?" she asked.

His hooded eyes looked at her. "Open the door."

Hesitantly, she obeyed. Behind her, he turned on the light.

She saw an enormous spartan bedroom, bigger than even the one in Texas. It had an enormous bed and a wall of windows covered with translucent curtains. There was a sitting area with a reading chair, a vanity table, a wet bar and a small library of books. Peeking into two side doors, she saw a large wood-paneled walk-in closet filled with dark suits, and an en suite bathroom in chrome and marble. The bathroom was so expensively minimalist that even the towels were tucked away.

Though this bedroom suite was huge and elegant, she

didn't see what could possibly make it more spectacular than the rooftop pool. Frowning, she turned back in puzzlement. "Your bedroom?"

He nodded.

"What do you love so much about it?"

Coming forward, he put his hands on her shoulders, his eyes alight. "That you'll be in it."

Belle shivered, remembering the heat and passion they'd shared at the Texas ranch. She wasn't hypocritical enough to pretend that the thought disgusted her. She bit her lip. "What would the staff think?"

He looked amused. "That I'd share my room with my pregnant fiancée? You think this will shock them?" He gave a low laugh. "Ah, *querida*, you are such an innocent. The servants think what I pay them to think."

She snorted, then paused. "Is that what you'll expect of me, too? That I'll just do what you tell me to do and think what you want me to think?"

His dark eyebrows lowered. "No." He pulled her into his arms, and ran his hand softly along her cheek. "You are not my servant, Belle. My expectations are different for you. I expect you to be yourself. And say what you actually think."

She looked at him skeptically. "You do?"

"Of course." His lips curved upward. "So I can convince you around to my way of thinking. The correct way."

She rolled her eyes. "Right."

"I have no interest in a silent doormat as a wife. I would rather have sparks between us, and yes, hatred at times, than be married to a ghost. I expect you to tell me when you are angry, rather than hide from me. You will be my wife and soon, the mother of my children…"

"Children?"

"Of course." He tilted his head. "You know how important siblings are. I was an only child. My life might have been very different if I'd had a sibling. Imagine how your younger brothers' lives might have turned out if they'd not had you to take care of them."

The thought gave her a chill. Her brothers would have been separated, sent to foster care. Or an orphanage, even, like Santiago. She bit her lip. "Of course it's important, but..."

"But?"

"This is all just so new to me. I feel like my life is already becoming unrecognizable. Planning a society wedding? Have more children? I don't know anything about running a mansion, or managing a staff."

"You will learn."

"I don't know about designer clothes, obviously—" she looked down at her stretchy *Bluebell Bears* T-shirt and shorts "—or elegant manners or..."

"I've arranged an appointment for you tomorrow at eleven with a personal stylist. Ivan will take you. Kip will go with you."

"Why would I need a bodyguard?"

"Consider him an accessory. You certainly won't be the only one with a bodyguard. Your stylist is..." He named a celebrity stylist so famous that even Belle had heard of her. "She'll provide you with clothes and everything else."

"Bodyguard. Stylist." She gave an incredulous, half-hysterical laugh. "I'm not some celebrity!"

"You are now, because of that ring on your finger." He gave her a slow, seductive smile. "As for the rest of what you'll need to learn, I'll teach as we go. It will get easier."

"How?" She was almost near tears. "How is this ever going to work?"

Reaching out, Santiago ran his hands down her arms, making her shiver with sudden awareness and desire as they stood in the shadowy bedroom.

"I'll show you," he whispered, drawing her to the enormous bed. "Starting with this."

And he kissed her.

Golden sunlight poured in through the high windows when Belle woke up the next morning. For a moment, she just stretched languorously in bed. She still felt him all over her body. Remembering last night curled her toes.

Then her smile faded as she realized she was waking up in New York just as she had in Texas: alone. His side of the bed was empty.

Last night, he'd made love to her so passionately he'd made all her fears disappear. She'd been lost in the sensuality of his body against hers. She'd felt need so hot and intense it burned everything else away.

But in the morning, reality felt as cold as his side of the bed.

Belle looked at the clock. It was ten in the morning. She sat up, eyes wide. She couldn't remember the last time she'd slept so late. Even in the earliest stages of pregnancy, when she'd been exhausted, she'd worked the early shift, forcing herself to get up at five on dark, cold winter mornings. She couldn't remember the last time she'd slept till ten. It felt sinful.

Rising from the bed, still naked as she'd slept, she stretched her arms and toes, and felt the baby kick inside her. She rubbed her belly, murmuring happily, "Good morning, baby."

Going to the en suite bathroom, she took a long, warm shower. Her meager belongings from her suitcases had already been unpacked. She wondered if it had been the butler or the maid who'd unpacked her clothes last night, when Santiago was giving her the house tour. She hoped it was the young maid. She felt uncomfortable at the thought of the supercilious butler looking down his nose at her simple clothing, all purchased from discount stores and washed many times.

"The servants think what I pay them to think," Santiago had told her grandly yesterday.

But Belle's own experience said otherwise. As a waitress, she'd been paid to serve breakfast and refill coffee; her opinion had always been her own. Her tart temper had gotten her in trouble more than once. Belle always believed in being polite, but that was different than letting a bully walk all over you.

"I have no interest in a silent doormat as a wife," he'd told her.

It was obviously true in bed. It was also true that in some ways, he made her feel stronger, braver and like she could really be herself, without pretending. But if Santiago thought Belle could ever be some kind of high society trophy wife, he'd soon realize his mistake. She was just afraid she'd humiliate all of them in the process.

After brushing out her wet hair, she pulled on a clean T-shirt and pair of shorts. They were getting too tight around her belly. Maybe a new wardrobe wasn't the worst idea, she thought. Brushing her teeth, she glanced at herself in the mirror. And heaven knew a stylist couldn't hurt. It would have to be a brave stylist, though, to want to take her on.

Ignoring the elevator—it seemed so pretentious—she went down the gleaming back stairs. She was just grateful Santiago had given her a house tour, or she'd have gotten totally lost. Approaching the kitchen, she heard a woman laugh.

"He can't be serious. We're really expected to follow her orders? That nobody? It's humiliating."

Sucking in her breath, Belle stopped outside the kitchen door, listening.

"Humiliating or not, we'll have to take her orders. At

least for now." The butler's voice was scornful. "However ridiculous they might be. Who knows what she might want?"

A different woman said, "A stripper pole?"

"Silver bowls full of pork rinds," the other suggested.

"But Mr. Velazquez has chosen her as his bride," the butler intoned, "so we must pretend to obey her for as long as the marriage lasts. But do not worry. Once the brat is born, she'll soon be kicked to the curb. Mr. Velazquez is seeing his lawyer today, hopefully drawing up an iron-clad prenup…"

Belle must have made some noise, because the butler's voice suddenly cut off. A second later, to her horror, his head peered around the door. Her own cheeks were aflame at being caught eavesdropping.

But Jones didn't look ashamed. If anything, his expression was smug, even as he said politely, "Ah, good morning, Miss Langtry. Would you care for some breakfast?"

Belle had no idea how to react. He knew she'd overheard, but wasn't remotely sorry. The butler was in charge here, not her, no matter what Santiago had said. Suddenly not the least bit hungry, she blurted out the first thing she thought of—the morning special she'd served at the diner. "Um…scrambled eggs and toast would be lovely… Maybe a little orange juice…"

"Of course, madam."

But as she walked forward with hunched shoulders, he blocked her from the kitchen, and gestured smoothly down the hall. "We will serve you in the dining room, Miss Langtry. There are newspapers and juice and coffee already set out. Please make yourself comfortable."

Comfortable was the last thing she felt as she ate alone at the end of a long table that would have seated twenty. Huge vases of fresh flowers made her nose itch, and she didn't find the *Financial Times* enough company to block out the memory of the staff's cruel words.

"Who knows what she might want?"

"A stripper's pole?"

"Silver bowls full of pork rinds?"

"She'll soon be kicked to the curb... Mr. Velazquez is seeing his lawyer today."

Santiago hadn't told her what his plans were today. He hadn't even said goodbye. He'd just made love to her hot and hard in the night, then disappeared before dawn. Like always.

Was he really with his lawyer right now, devising some kind of ironclad prenuptial agreement?

Of course he was, she thought bitterly. He wouldn't trust her, ever. That was what their marriage would be, in spite of all his fine words about friendship and partnership. It would be a business arrangement, based on a contract, where even the people running her own home despised her.

This mansion wasn't home, she thought with despair, looking up at the soaring chandeliers, the high ceilings of the dining room. She didn't belong here. She rubbed her belly. Neither did her baby.

She missed her brothers. She missed Letty, who was in Greece with her family. She missed her old friends back in Bluebell. Most of all, she missed having control over her life.

Why would any woman want to get pregnant by a billionaire, if it meant you'd always feel like an outsider? Would even her own child, raised in this environment, someday despise her?

Jones served her breakfast on a silver tray, then departed with a sweeping bow. But Belle saw his smirk. She managed to eat a few bites, but it all tasted like ash in her mouth. She was relieved when Kip, the muscular, tattooed bodyguard, appeared in the doorway.

"Ready to go, Miss Langtry? Ivan has already pulled around the car."

Belle had dreaded the thought of the appointment with that famous personal stylist, but at that moment hell itself sounded preferable to remaining in this enormous, empty house, filled with employees who scorned her. She got up from the breakfast table so quickly that Kip's eyes widened to see a pregnant woman move so fast.

But later that afternoon, when Belle finally returned to the house, she felt worse, not better. She'd been poked and prodded, manicured and, most of all, criticized. Her awful hair! Her awful clothes! Her ragged cuticles! The famous stylist had cried out in shock and agony, right in front of Belle, and sent her assistants scurrying. They seemed to think Belle was a rock, incapable of thinking or feeling, just the brute clay from which they, the long-suffering artists, would sculpt and construct their art.

Ten different assistants had worked on her at the stylist's private salon, which the stylist herself, the famous owner of the establishment, called her *atelier*.

Belle had never cared much about her appearance. She'd always had more important things to think about, like raising her little brothers and putting food on the table. So she'd tried to remain patient and silent as they picked out a wardrobe and hairstyle appropriate to her station as a rich man's wife.

Seven hours later, as Kip finally carried out her new wardrobe to the waiting car, the famous stylist had showed Belle a mirror. "What do you think?"

She'd sucked in her breath. Her dark hair was now perfectly straight, gleaming down her shoulders. Her face felt raw from the facials, shellacked with expensive lotions and makeup, including lipstick and mascara. Her pregnant shape was draped in a severely chic black shift dress, black capelet, her hips thrust forward by uncomfortably high heels.

Startled by the stranger in the mirror, Belle replied timidly, "I don't recognize myself."

To which the famously pretentious personal stylist responded with a laugh, "Then my job is done."

Now, Belle trudged into the brownstone mansion feeling ridiculous in the jaunty black capelet.

Tomorrow she was supposed to meet with the wedding planner. She could only imagine how that would go. Santiago had already mentioned an engagement party he meant to hold in two weeks, "after you've gotten a chance to get comfortable." Comfortable?

She felt sick with worry.

Belle saw the maid and the cook as she walked wearily into the house. The two women elbowed each other as they saw her new chic appearance.

"You look nice, ma'am," the maid said meekly. Belle wondered if she was mocking her.

"Thank you," she said flatly, and went up to the third floor bedroom suite to take a nap. The same maid knocked on the door a few hours later.

"Mr. Velazquez is home, miss. He's requesting that you join him downstairs for dinner."

Groggily, Belle smoothed down her dress and hair from her nap, then went down to the dining room.

Santiago's dark eyes widened when he saw her. Rising from the table, he came forward to kiss her.

"You look very elegant," he said, helping her into her chair. Sitting beside her, he smiled. "Who is queen of society now?"

He didn't seem to notice her lack of enthusiasm or her absence of appetite for dinner. But there was one thing he noticed fast enough. When he took her upstairs to bed and kissed her, she didn't respond. He frowned. "What is it?"

"It's this makeup," she improvised. "It feels like a Halloween mask over my face."

He stared at her, then gave her a slow-rising grin. "I can solve that."

He pulled her into the shower, turned on the water, and scrubbed the day off her until she felt almost like herself again. It was only then, when her skin was pink and warm with steam, as she stood in front of him with her baby bump and pregnancy-swollen breasts, that she felt like she could breathe again, and started returning his kisses.

"That's better," he whispered appreciatively and kissed her in the shower until her knees were weak. Turning off the water, he gently toweled her off and pulled her onto the bed, their bodies still hot and wet. Lying down, he lifted her over him and put his hand gently on her cheek.

"You're in charge," he whispered, and she was. It was ecstasy. It was glory. Their souls seemed to spark together into fire, as well as their bodies. When they were together in bed, she could forget all her fears. She felt nothing but pleasure. She was his. He was hers.

But when Belle woke up in the morning, she was alone.

CHAPTER SIX

Two weeks later, Santiago came home from his forty-floor skyscraper in Midtown with a scowl on his face.

His company, Velazquez International, had spent two weeks in negotiations, trying and failing to nail down the acquisition of a Canadian hotel chain. He'd offered them an excellent price, but they continued to hold out—not for more money, but for his promise that he'd keep all their employees and stores intact. Santiago scowled, narrowing his eyes. What fool would promise such a thing? But now, because of their stubbornness, he was going to be late for his own engagement party. And no deal had been struck.

That was what was making him tense, he told himself. The business deal. Running late.

It had nothing to do with the thought of giving Belle the prenuptial agreement tucked into his briefcase.

Rushing up the stone steps of his brownstone, he ground his teeth. The wedding was planned for early September, just a month away, just a few weeks before her due date. Of course the agreement had to be signed. He was a billionaire. Belle had nothing. Without a prenuptial agreement, he'd be risking half his fortune from the moment he said "I do."

But his scowl deepened as he entered his Upper East Side mansion, lavish with flowers and additional hired serving staff, awaiting the first guest for their engagement party, when he would introduce his future bride to New

York society. He took the elevator to the third floor, then stopped when he saw Belle.

She was looking into a full-length mirror as she put on diamond earrings, wearing a sleek black dress, her dark hair pulled back into a tight chignon. Her face was perfectly made up, and the diamond earrings he'd given her yesterday sparkled as brightly as the ten-carat engagement ring on her finger. But as she turned to him, he saw that beneath the dramatic black sweep of her lashes and red ruby lips, her creamy caramel skin was pale.

"What's wrong?" he demanded.

She gave him a trembling smile. "I was starting to worry you might make me host this party alone."

"Of course not." Dropping his briefcase, he kissed her, stroking her soft cheek. He searched her gaze. "You look beautiful."

"I'm glad. So maybe the pain is worth it."

"Pain?" he said, surprised.

She held out her foot, shod in a sexy black stiletto heel. "And you should see my underwear," she said wryly.

"I'd like to."

She returned his grin, then sighed. "At least the baby is comfortable. All the clothes are loose around my waist." She glanced down at the briefcase. "So when are you going to spring it on me?"

His hand stilled. "What?"

"The prenuptial agreement."

He blinked. How had she known?

Of course she knew, he chided himself. Belle was intuitive and smart. "You know it's necessary."

"Yes. I know."

She didn't argue. Didn't complain. She just looked at him, her dark eyes like big pools in her wan, pale face. And he felt like a cad. That irritated him even more. Turning away, he changed his clothes, pulling on his tuxedo.

"Santiago, am I a trophy wife?" she asked suddenly.

"What are you talking about?"

"I met some other brides while waiting for my appointment with the wedding planner yesterday. They told me all about the life of a trophy wife. They made it sound like being an indentured servant." She looked at the closet. "I already have the uniform. Shift dresses in black and beige."

He felt irritated as he sat down on the bed to put on his Italian leather shoes. "I didn't tell you to only wear black and beige."

"No, but the stylist did. And she insisted I must always wear stilettos, to be taller. They're like torture devices…" She peered down at her feet, then looked up with a sigh. "I'll sorry. I'm doing my best. I'm just afraid I'll fail you," she said in a small voice. "That I can't be what you need, or ever fit into your world—"

"Fit in?" He looked up from tying his shoes. "I wasn't born in this world either, Belle. Growing up in Madrid, I had nothing. And I've learned the hard way there's only one way to fit into a world that doesn't want you. By force. You have to make it impossible for them to ignore you."

She stared at him for a moment, and he wished he hadn't brought up his own childhood. He was relieved when she shook her head. "Force? I can't even force our wedding planner to consider any of my ideas. Our wedding is going to be awful."

"Awful?"

Belle rolled her eyes. "She called it 'postmodern'. I'm to hold a cactus instead of a bouquet, and instead of a white wedding cake, we'll be serving our guests gold-dusted foam."

"Really."

"When I told her I didn't want to hold a cactus in my bare hands and just wanted a wildflower bouquet and a regular wedding cake, the woman laughed and patted me on the head. She *patted me on the head*," she repeated for emphasis.

Santiago gave a low laugh. "*Querida*, her weddings might be unconventional, but she is the best, and I told her I want you to have the most spectacular wedding of the season…"

"*Spectacular* means wasting millions of dollars on stupid stuff we don't want, to impress people we don't even like?"

"You said you want to fit in. A big wedding is a show of power."

"She won't even let me invite my brothers. She said it was because she didn't think a plumber and a fireman would be comfortable at such a formal event, but I think she was just afraid they wouldn't fit in with her décor!"

Not letting Belle invite her little brothers? He was willing to accept cactus and gold foam, but excluding beloved family members was unacceptable. Santiago frowned as he finished putting on his tie. "I'll talk to her." Rising to his feet, he held out his arm. "Shall we go downstairs?"

He felt her hands shake a little as they wrapped around the arm of his jacket, heard the sudden catch of her breath. "So many guests are coming tonight…"

"It will be fine," he said, but he understood why Belle was nervous. Their 'impromptu engagement party' had ballooned out of proportion. On August weekends, the city usually was so deserted he wouldn't have been half-surprised to see tumbleweeds going down Fifth Avenue. But to his surprise, everyone they'd invited had instantly accepted. Not only that, but more had asked to come, even coming in from Connecticut and the Hamptons.

Everyone, it seemed, was curious to see the pregnant Texas waitress who'd tamed the famous playboy Santiago Velazquez.

"Gossip has spread about me," Belle said glumly.

"Ignore it."

"The butler's right, I'm nobody."

"So was I, when I came to America at eighteen," Santiago pointed out.

"That just adds to your glory," she said grumpily. "Now you're a self-made billionaire. I bet you've never failed at anything."

That wasn't true. Just five years ago, Santiago had failed in spectacular fashion.

But he wasn't going to tell Belle about Nadia. Not now. Not ever.

Pushing the button for the elevator, he turned to her with a sudden frown. "What did you mean, the butler was right? Did he say something to you?"

Averting her eyes, she nodded. "I overheard the butler and cook and maid talking a couple weeks ago. They weren't happy about having me as their mistress. Mr. Jones told them I was a nobody, but they should pretend to obey me until the *brat* was born, when you'd get rid of me."

"What?"

"He knew I heard them talking, but wasn't even sorry." Lifting her gaze, she tried to smile. "It's no big deal. I'll get used to it."

But Santiago's jaw was tight with fury. That his own employees would dare to scorn his future wife, his unborn child, in his own house! His dark brows lowered like a thundercloud.

Once the elevator opened on the ground floor, he took Belle by the arm and led her down the hall, past all the extra hired staff who were setting out appetizers and flowers for the party.

In the kitchen, he found the butler busy with preparations for the meal, along with the two other live-in members of his staff—Mrs. Green, the cook, and Anna, the maid. The front doorbell rang, and the butler started to leave the kitchen.

"Jones, stay," Santiago ordered harshly, then turned to one of the temporary waiters walking past with a tray. "Tell Kip he's in charge of answering the door."

"Kip?"

"The one with a tattoo on his neck."

"Right."

Santiago turned back to face his employees.

"What is it, Mr. Velazquez?" Anna said anxiously.

"I should be answering the door for your party guests, Mr. Velazquez," Jones intoned.

Santiago looked at the three of them coldly.

"You are all fired."

They stared at him in shock, their mouths agape.

"Pack up your things," Santiago continued grimly. "I want you out of here in ten minutes."

"But—my food for the party—" Mrs. Green stammered.

"What did we do?" Anna gasped.

"You told him to fire us." The butler looked at Belle with venom in his eyes. "You just had to tattle, didn't you?"

"I never meant for this to happen…" Belle looked at Santiago. She put an urgent hand on his shoulder. "Please. You don't need to—"

But he moved his shoulder away. His fury was past listening as he stared at the three employees who'd dared to be rude to Belle. "This party is no longer your concern, and you now only have nine minutes left."

The butler drew himself up contemptuously. "I'll go. It would destroy my professional reputation to work for your wife, anyway. She doesn't belong here!"

"You think your reputation would be destroyed?" Santiago said coldly. "See what happens if you ever speak rudely about Belle again to anyone."

"Santiago," Belle said, tugging on his sleeve desperately. "I don't want anyone to lose their jobs. I just thought…"

"I should have known you'd rat us out, after you heard us talking that first day," Jones snarled.

The plump cook whirled to Belle with a gasp. "You heard us?"

But Belle was staring at the butler, and so was Santiago. So was the maid.

Jones's accent had slipped.

Suddenly Santiago knew why the butler had hated Belle on sight. She wasn't the only one who felt out of place.

"You're not even British," Santiago said accusingly.

"Nope." Jones yanked off the apron that had been over his suit and tie. "Born in New Jersey. I'm done with this butler stuff. No amount of money is worth this." He looked at Belle. "You might be stuck here till he dumps you. But I'm not. Forget this. I'm going to go start a band."

Throwing away his apron, he left.

Santiago looked at the two women. "Any last words?"

The young maid, Anna, turned to Belle, her cheeks red. "I'm sorry, Miss Langtry. I sneered at you about pork rinds because, well, I like them myself. But I eat them in secret. I didn't want Mr. Jones to know… "

The cook stepped forward, abashed. "And I taunted you about the stripper pole, because, well—" the plump middle-aged woman's cheeks reddened "—I was a stripper myself for a few months when I was young. It's not something I'm proud of, but my baby's father had abandoned us. I was desperate…" Turning to Santiago, she pulled off her cap. "That bit of employment wasn't listed on my résumé. I understand if you don't want me cooking for you no more. Especially after what I said. I'll go."

"Please don't fire me," Anna begged. "I need this job.

I'm working my way through law school and the hours are hard to find. The wages, too."

"It's not your choice." Santiago looked at Belle. "It's my fiancée's."

Belle glanced at the two women. The younger of them was looking at her with pleading eyes, as the older stared woodenly at the floor with slumped shoulders.

"Please stay." Her voice trembled slightly. "If you're not too embarrassed to work for me…"

"Oh, no!" Anna exclaimed fervently. "How could I be embarrassed of you? I'm only ashamed of myself."

"Me, too," the cook said softly. Looking up, her soft blue eyes filled with tears. "Thank you."

Belle gave them a wobbly smile. "I know what it feels like to be pregnant and alone. No one would judge you badly for doing whatever it took to take care of your baby." Glancing at Santiago out of the corner of her eye, she added, "In fact, you both get a raise."

"What?" the women said joyfully.

"Of thirty percent!"

"What?" Santiago said, not so joyfully.

"A raise," Belle repeated firmly, "as our household will be doing without a butler. Their extra responsibilities deserve it."

She made a good point. Santiago scowled at her. And he had to admit to himself that having a butler, especially a sniffy one like Jones, hadn't added much to the comfort of his home life.

"Fine," he said grudgingly, then turned to the others. "Don't give my bride reason to regret her generosity. There will be no second chance."

"Yes, sir!"

"Back to your duties."

"Right away!"

Mrs. Green scurried back to the enormous ovens, her plump face alarmed. "Oh, no—my salmon puffs!"

Taking Belle aside in the hallway, he growled, "Thirty percent?"

She lifted her chin. "They will be worth it."

"Right. And here I thought the most expensive thing would be getting you a new wardrobe."

"What about this?" She smiled, lifting up the huge diamond ring on her left hand. "I can't even imagine how much it cost."

Try free, he thought. He cleared his throat, then brightened. "And your earrings." Those, at least, had been specifically purchased for Belle.

She touched one of the diamonds dangling from her ears. "You could have bought me fake ones, you know. No one would have been able to tell the difference, least of all me. Big waste of money."

"You really are terrible at being a gold digger."

"I know," she agreed. She looked down at her ring. "It's beautiful, but it makes me feel guilty. This ring could have probably bought a car."

When he'd bought it five years before, the amount he'd spent could actually have bought a house. But of course he'd bought it for a different woman, so Belle had nothing to feel guilty about. He was tempted to tell her, but kept his mouth shut. Somehow he thought this was one situation when no woman on earth, even an ardent environmentalist, would think highly of recycling.

The doorbell rang again, and he saw the seven-foot-tall Kip head for the front door. Flinging it open, Kip glared at an ambassador, who looked startled, and his skinny, bejeweled wife, who looked terrified.

"Oh, dear," Belle sighed, following his gaze.

"I'm not sure Kip has the right skill set to be butler," Santiago said, hiding a smile.

"Let's go take over for him."

He frowned at her. "Answer the door ourselves?"

"What, don't you know how?" Giving him an impish smile, she took his hand. "Come on, Santiago. Let's give 'em a big Texas welcome."

Her hand was warm in his own, and as he looked down at the curve of her breasts revealed above the neckline of her gown, a flash of heat went through his body. "I thought you were afraid of society people."

"I am." She added with a rueful laugh, "But my mama always said there's only one way to get through something that scares you, and that's by doing it."

Looking at the resolve in Belle's beautiful face, at the gleam in her dark eyes and her half-parted ruby-red lips, Santiago was tempted to give her a counteroffer: that they throw all the guests out, lock the door, and make love right here, on the table between the flowers and the cream puffs.

Instead, as the doorbell rang again, Belle pulled him toward the door.

"I just fired Jones," Santiago told Kip. "Make sure he doesn't make off with the silver."

"Yes, sir," Kip said, looking relieved, and he fled.

Santiago stood beside Belle as they answered the door, welcoming all their illustrious, powerful guests. The people were all strangers to Belle, and yet she gave each of them a warm smile, as if she were truly glad to see them. Some of the guests seemed pleased, others slightly startled.

Santiago was enchanted.

Over the next few hours, as he watched Belle mingle at the party, he felt a mixture of pride and desire. He couldn't take his eyes off her. She was breathtaking.

In that dress and those high heels, with her makeup and hair so glossy and sophisticated, she might have fit in perfectly, except for one thing.

She stood out.

Belle was the most beautiful woman there.

Only he knew the fear and insecurity she'd hidden inside. That somehow made him even prouder of her. Tonight he admired her courage and grace even more than he admired her beauty.

The house had been filled with bright-colored flowers, and the hors d'oeuvres, overseen by Mrs. Green, were exquisite. But not half as exquisite as Belle, feverishly bright-eyed and lovely. The party was a huge success.

Because of Belle, he thought. She was the star.

Later that evening, he watched her across the crowded ballroom, now smiling at three of the board members of the Canadian hotel chain. He'd invited them to the party in an offhand way, but he hadn't really expected them to come. He watched as Belle smiled and said something that made all three men laugh uproariously.

Belle was as good at this as Nadia, he thought in astonishment. Maybe even better.

He'd met Nadia his first night at the orphanage in Madrid, when he was fourteen. She was blonde, beautiful, a year older, with hard violet eyes and a raspy laugh. He'd been immediately infatuated. When he told her he was breaking out to go live with his father, the Duke of Sangovia, she'd been awed. "Take me with you," she'd begged, and he'd agreed.

Nadia had watched from the bushes as the palace guards tried phoning his father, then at the duke's answer, turned on Santiago scornfully, setting the dogs on him. He'd run away from the snarling jaws and snapping teeth, staggering past the safety of the gate, to fall at her feet.

"No luck, huh?" Nadia had said, looking down at him coolly. She'd looked past the wrought-iron walls, ten feet tall, over the palm trees, toward the rooftops of the palace, barely visible from the gate. "Someday, I'll live in a place like this."

"I won't." Wiping blood from his face, Santiago had looked back at it with hatred, then slowly risen to his feet, ignoring the blood on his knees, the rips in his pants. "My house will be a million times better than this." He'd looked at the beautiful blonde girl. "And you'll be my wife."

"Marry you?" She'd looked at him coolly. "I'm going to be a movie star. There's no reason I'd marry you or anyone. Not unless you could give me something I can't get for myself." Her lovely face was thoughtful as she looked back toward the palace. "If you could make me a duchess…"

That was one thing Santiago could never do. He wasn't the legitimate heir. He was just a bastard by-blow, whose father couldn't be bothered to give him a home, a name, or even a single minute of his time. A sliver of pain went through him, overwhelmed by a wave of rage.

He would be better than his father. Better than his half brother. Better than all of them.

Lifting his chin, he'd said boldly, "Someday, I'll be a billionaire. Then I'll ask you. And you'll say yes."

Nadia had given a low, patronizing laugh. "A billionaire?" she'd said, putting out her cigarette. "Sure. Ask me then."

He'd officially made his first billion by the time he was thirty. But too late. The day his company went public, he flew his private jet to Barcelona, where Nadia was filming her latest movie. He'd fallen to one knee and held out the ring, just as he'd imagined for half his life. And then he'd waited.

One never knew where one stood with Nadia. She knew how to charm with a glance, how to cut out someone's heart with a smile. Sitting on her film set, looking beautiful as a queen, she'd fluttered her eyelashes mournfully.

"Oh, dear. I'm sorry. You're too late. I just agreed to marry your brother." She'd held out her left hand, showing off an exquisite antique ring. "I'm going to live in the

Palacio de las Palmas and be a duchess someday. I can only do that if I marry the Duque de Sangovia's legitimate heir. And that's not you. Sorry."

Strange to think that Nadia was living with his father and brother, Santiago thought, while he himself had never met either of them. Nadia had been married to his brother for five years now, and as she waited to be duchess she comforted herself with the title of *marquesa*, along with the other title given her by the European tabloids—"the Most Beautiful Woman in the World."

"Hell of a girl you've got there."

Coming out of his reverie, Santiago abruptly focused on the man speaking to him. It was Rob McVoy, the CEO of the Canadian family firm. "Thank you."

"Any man who could make a woman like Belle love him must be trustworthy. So I changed my mind. We'll take the chance." He gave a brusque nod. "We agree to the deal."

Santiago blinked in shock. "You do?"

The man clapped him on the shoulder. "Our lawyers will be in touch."

Santiago stared after him in amazement. After weeks of stalled negotiations, accusations of double-dealing and an almost total lack of trust, the Canadians were suddenly willing to sell him their family company, just after spending twenty minutes talking to Belle?

He was still in shock hours later, when the appetizers and champagne were almost gone, the flowers starting to wilt and the last guests straggling out. Belle had already gone upstairs. As a pregnant woman, no one thought less of her for being tired, and they'd all said goodbye to her with fond, indulgent smiles. Santiago was amazed. How had she become so popular with so many, so fast?

Not with everyone, of course. Some of the trophy wives and girlfriends, some of the more shallow hedge fund billionaires, had indeed looked askance, and whispered behind their hands, smirking.

Everyone else had loved her.

Going to the third floor, Santiago found her in their bedroom, sitting on their bed, her shoes kicked off. His gaze swept over the curves of her breasts as she leaned over to rub her bare feet, wincing. "These shoes. Murder!"

Dropping his tuxedo jacket and tie to the floor, he sat beside her on the enormous bed. Pulling her feet into his lap, he started massaging them.

"That feels fantastic," she murmured. Her eyes closed in pleasure as she leaned back against the pillows.

"Did you enjoy the party?" It took several moments for her to answer.

"Um. It was great."

He stopped rubbing her feet. "How was it really?"

With a sigh, she opened her eyes.

"Fine?" she tried, and it was even less believable. He snorted.

"You really are the worst actress I've ever seen," he observed. He started rubbing the arches of her feet, and she exhaled in pleasure.

"All right, it wasn't easy. Those shoes are like instruments of death. And people kept talking about things I didn't understand—effective altruism as related to overnight borrowing rates, for example..."

"Those aren't at all related."

She glared at him in irritation. "That's exactly my point. I don't know, and don't care." She yawned. "Then others started discussing the gallery show of an artist I never heard of. When I confessed as much, they were horrified and said you owned one of his paintings. Then they made me go take a look at it."

"Which painting?"

"The—um... Mira?"

"Joan Miró?"

"Yeah. They said you'd gotten it at a steal for ten million dollars. I barely restrained myself from yelping, 'That squiggle? I've seen better art done by preschoolers!'" Shaking her head, she added defensively, "And I have."

"Very diplomatic to restrain yourself from saying so."

"Took a lot of willpower, I'll tell you."

He smiled. "You were amazing tonight. Every time I glanced over at you, whomever you were talking to looked enthralled."

She blushed shyly. "Really? You're just being kind."

"Excuse me, have we met?"

She smiled. "Well, I tried my best. Any time I felt nervous, I forced myself to smile and say something nice, like my mama taught me. You know, 'Beautiful dress!' 'What a lovely necklace!'"

"What about the men? Did you compliment their neckties?"

She fluttered her dark eyelashes coyly. "I brought up football, or if that didn't work, horses. You apparently know a lot of polo players. As a last resort, politics."

"Do you follow politics?" he said, surprised.

"Not at all. But generally if you just start the ball rolling, the other person's happy to take it and run. At that point, all you have to do is make sympathetic noises." She rubbed the back of her neck and yawned again. "I'm exhausted. This must be what it's like to act in a play all night. The role of trophy wife."

"You closed a multi-million-dollar deal, Belle."

She frowned. "What?"

"The McVoys…"

She brightened. "Oh, the guys from Calgary? They were hilarious. They were talking about this action movie they saw last night, with that Spanish movie star, you know, the famous one…" She rolled her eyes. "I think they have a crush on her. She's married to some kind of prince already, but I told the guys it never hurts to dream." She gave a sudden grin. "Movie stars get married and divorced dozens of times, don't they? And you never know. She might decide what she really wants next is a middle-aged Canadian with hockey skills."

Santiago's body felt like ice. He cleared his throat. "I've been negotiating with the McVoys for weeks, trying to buy their company." His voice was still a little hoarse. He forced his lips into a smile. "They just agreed to the deal only because of you."

"Me?" she said, astonished.

"They said any man you love couldn't be all bad."

"Oh." Her cheeks went red as she said quickly, "I never told them I loved you."

"I guess they just assumed, since we're getting married and all," he said dryly. "Turn around." Reaching out, he started massaging the back of her neck, her shoulders, brushing back the dark tendrils of her hair. As she leaned against his hands, he breathed in the scent of her, like vanilla and orange blossoms.

She leaned back, looking at him over her shoulder. "Can I ask you something?"

"You'll ask it, whether I say yes or no."

"You're right." She flashed him a sudden grin, then grew serious. "What turned you against the idea of love?"

His hands stilled on her shoulders.

"I told you about my parents."

"That wasn't all, was it? There was something else. Someone else." She took a deep breath, and raised her eyes pleadingly to his. "You know about my sad romantic history, but I know nothing about yours...."

"You're right," he said slowly. "There was a woman."

Belle sat up straight. He saw that he had her full attention. He wasn't sure why he was telling her this. He'd never spoken about it to anyone.

"When I was a teenager, I met a girl in the orphanage. She was blonde, beautiful, with violet eyes..." He tensed, remembering how he'd felt about her as a boy. "She was older than me. Street-smart. Brave. We both had such big dreams about the future. We were both going to conquer the world." He gave a humorless smile. "At fourteen, I asked her to marry me. She told me to ask her again after I proved myself. So I did."

"How?"

"I earned a billion-dollar fortune. For her."

Her eyes went wide. "What?"

Santiago turned away, his jaw tight. "It took me sixteen years, but when my company went public five years ago, I went to Spain with a huge diamond ring."

His eyes fell unwillingly to Belle's left hand, but fortunately she didn't notice. Sitting across from him on the bed, she was staring at him with wide eyes.

"What happened?" she breathed.

His lips twisted at the edges. "I came too late. She wanted more than I could give her. She'd just gotten engaged to my brother."

Her expression changed to horror. "Your *brother*?"

He gave a crooked half grin. "She told me that she'd been attracted to Otilio in part because he reminded her of me. An upgraded version of me." His voice held no emotion. He'd had a lot of practice at showing none. Feeling none. "I couldn't even begrudge her choice. Marrying into the official Zoya family meant she would not be merely rich, but famous and powerful across Europe, and someday, after my father is dead, a duchess."

"Of all men on earth—your brother!"

"Their marriage was a huge social event in Madrid, I heard later."

"What a horrible woman!" she cried indignantly. Her lovely heart-shaped face was stricken as she faced him across the shadowy bed. "No wonder you think so little of love. And marriage, too. What did you do, after she told you she was marrying your brother?"

He shrugged. "I came back to New York. I worked harder. My fortune is bigger than theirs now. The Zoya family owns an *estancia* in Argentina, so I bought a bigger ranch in Texas. They have an art collection. Now mine is better. I don't need them now. They're nothing to me."

"They're your family," she said forlornly.

"They chose not to be."

Reaching out, Belle put her arms around him, hugging him close to her on the bed, offering comfort. For a moment, he accepted the warmth of her smaller body cradled against his. He exhaled deeply. He hadn't even realized his jaw had been tense, until now, as the tension melted away. Drawing back, he looked down at her, and gently tucked a dark tendril of hair back into her loose chignon.

She'd offered him comfort tonight, and loyalty, and her charm had even helped him close a business deal. She'd given it all without asking for anything in return.

He wanted to show his appreciation. Give her a present. But she wouldn't care about jewelry or clothes or art. *Especially* not art, he thought with amusement. So what?

Then he knew.

"I'll cancel the wedding planner, Belle. We can have any kind of wedding you want."

Her eyes lit up. It was worth it for that alone. She breathed, "Really?"

"I know you'll want your brothers to attend. I'll send my private jet to collect them. We don't have to hold the ceremony at the cathedral. I don't care about the details." He looked at her. "As long as we are husband and wife before our child comes into this world."

She tilted her head thoughtfully. "What about having the wedding here?"

"Here?"

She nodded eagerly. "I can have a flower bouquet, instead of holding a cactus. A real cake, instead of foam." She was beaming. "We can have good food that people might actually want to eat!"

"Ah, Belle." With a low laugh, he drew her closer on the bed, cupping her face. "Forget what I said about fitting in. You will never fit in." She looked hurt. Still smiling, he reached out and gently lifted her chin. "Because you were born to stand out, *querida*. You were the most beautiful woman at our engagement party. No one could even compare. I couldn't take my eyes off you."

Her cheeks flushed with shy pleasure. "Really?"

"Just one thing is wrong. That dress." He ran his hand along the black fabric. "It's driving me crazy."

Belle checked the back zipper self-consciously. "What's wrong with it?"

Sitting next to her on the bed, he pulled her into his arms.

"That you're still wearing it," he whispered, and lowered his mouth to hers.

CHAPTER SEVEN

For Santiago, sex had always been simple. Easy. A quick release. A brief pleasure, swiftly forgotten.

Sex with Belle was different than he'd ever experienced before. It was fire. A conflagration. A drug he could not get enough of.

But as with any drug, he was soon hit by unwanted, bewildering side effects.

Having Belle in his Upper East Side mansion, in his bed every night, he was shocked by the way their nighttime pleasures started to bleed into his days. He could not refuse her anything.

First, he'd agreed to change their wedding, even though the celebration the famous wedding planner had proposed would have been the social event of the year. The wedding Belle wanted, small and private, without pomp or press coverage, would do nothing for the prestige of his name.

But he let Belle have her way. And it didn't stop there.

He found himself thinking about her during the daylight hours, when his focus was supposed to be on running his company. The Canadian deal had gone through, but other deals began to fall apart. He was distracted, and it was affecting his business. He found himself impatient, even bored, at meetings—even when he himself was the one who'd called them.

He'd spent almost twenty years focused on building Velazquez International to be a huge multinational conglomerate, owning a host of brands of everything from food and soft drinks to running shoes and five-star resorts. He'd spent the last five years at an almost obsessive expansion, buying up small companies with an eye to a future where he owned the world.

But now, as he signed documents to purchase his latest company, a valuable nutritional supplement firm based in Copenhagen, instead of triumph he felt only irritation.

He didn't give a damn about vitamins or protein powders. He wanted to be home with Belle. In her arms. In her bed.

And it was getting worse. At night, when he was in her arms, lost in her deep, expressive brown eyes, kissing her sensual mouth, he'd started to feel something he'd sworn he never would again. Something more than desire.

He found himself caring about her opinion.

He found himself...caring.

In daylight, the thought chilled Santiago to the bone. He couldn't let himself be vulnerable. He'd be marrying her in a matter of weeks, and soon afterward, they'd be raising a child together.

Marriage he could justify, as a mere piece of paper to secure his child's name.

But actually caring about Belle...

Needing her happiness...

Needing *her*...

That was something else.

He could never risk the devastation of loving someone again. He couldn't be that stupid. He couldn't.

But as the weeks passed and their wedding date approached, Santiago grew increasingly tense. Every day he was with Belle, every night, he felt intimacy building between them. The wedding he'd once insisted upon now started to feel like a ticking time bomb. Waiting to explode. To destroy.

It made him want to run.

I made a promise, he told himself desperately. *To Belle. To our child. I'm not going anywhere.*

But as their wedding grew closer, his fears intensified. No matter how much he tried to shove down his feelings. No matter how he tried to deny them.

I have to marry her. For my child's sake. It's just a piece of paper. Not my soul!

But the closer their wedding date became, the more edgy he felt.

Belle woke before dawn on her wedding day, and when she opened her eyes in the gray September light, she looked across the bed. A smile burst across her face brighter than the sun.

It was an omen. Today was their wedding day. And it was the first time she hadn't woken alone.

Santiago was sleeping in bed beside her.

With a rush of gratitude, Belle smiled to herself happily, listening to his deep breathing beside her in the shadows of their bedroom.

After all her fears and plans, she would marry him tonight. And just in time, since at three weeks from her due date, her belly had gotten so huge that she barely fit into her simple, pretty wedding dress. Tonight, in a candlelight ceremony on their rooftop garden, she would officially become Mrs. Santiago Velazquez.

The past month in New York had been filled with unexpected joys, like fixing up this house. It hadn't been a makeover, but a make-*under*. Seven stories, elevator, rooftop garden, wine cellar and all, it had become a real home as she believed a home should be: comfy and cozy. She'd softened the cold, stark modern design, replacing the angular furniture with plump sofas that you could cuddle in.

The master closet, sadly, was now full of fashionable,

scratchy black dresses and stiletto heels, but on the plus side, if she still hated going out into society, at least she loved coming home.

This house had somehow become her home.

After their rocky start, she'd become friends with the live-in staff—Dinah Green, the cook, and Anna Phelps, the maid. Belle often helped them with their tasks, just for the company, and because she liked taking care of her own home. She'd helped Anna study for tests for law school. Dinah had taught her some delicious new recipes, and Belle had already volunteered to cook on every holiday so the older woman could have the time off to visit her grown-up son in Philadelphia.

Together, the three women had worked together to plan everything for the wedding tonight.

It would be a simple affair, a short ceremony attended by family and friends, followed by a late dinner. A judge friend of Santiago's was going to officiate. They already had the marriage license. Afterward, there would be a sit-down dinner of roast beef and grilled asparagus on the rooftop desk, then dancing to music provided by a jazz trio, cake and champagne toasts, and all done by midnight.

Planning the event hadn't been too hard. Belle wasn't that picky, and besides, she'd discovered that living on the Upper East Side, with a driver and unlimited money, was an entirely different New York experience from when she'd shared a walk-up apartment and struggled to make the bills in Brooklyn.

Here, she had a concierge obstetrician who made house calls. Here, she had time. Here, she had space. Her heart fluttered when Santiago came home each night, and they ate dinner together at the long table. He was very busy with his company and often worked long days. But on weekends he would take her out to little cafés—which she enjoyed— and trendy restaurants—which she didn't.

He'd taken her to see a certain famous musical sold out on Broadway, with front-row tickets that the whole world knew were impossible to get. Sitting next to him in the audience that night, Belle realized that she wasn't wishing she could trade places with the actress on stage. She liked where she was, at Santiago's side, with his hand resting protectively on her baby bump. She'd looked at him in the darkened theater. Feeling her look, he'd squeezed her hand.

Then, a minute later, he'd abruptly dropped it.

It was strange. One minute she felt so close to him, as their eyes met in mutual understanding, or a shared joke. But the next minute, he would suddenly seem distant, or literally leave the room. She didn't know which was worse.

Maybe he was having annoyances at work. Maybe he was nervous about their baby's upcoming due date, in just three weeks. She could hardly wait to meet their baby and hold her in their arms.

She intended to have their baby sleep in a bassinet next to their bed at first, but she'd already decorated the nursery to be ready. It was a sweet room, with pale pink walls, a crystal chandelier, a pretty white crib, changing table and rocking chair. And a huge stuffed white polar bear in the corner.

That stuffed bear, twelve feet tall, had been brought home yesterday by Santiago, carried into the nursery with the assistance of Kip.

Belle had laughed. "And you say you have no idea how to be a father. Didn't they have a bigger one?"

"I'm glad they didn't. I would have had to bring it in with a crane through the window. It barely fit in the elevator."

"You're a genius," she'd proclaimed, kissing him happily. "And to think all I've done today for the baby is look through the baby name book."

"Find anything?"

"Well, maybe," she said shyly. He seemed in such a good mood, she'd ventured, "What would you think about naming her Emma Valeria, after both our mothers?"

Santiago's expression immediately turned cold.

"Name her after your mother, if you like. Keep mine out of it."

And he'd abruptly left the nursery.

She shivered. He was always going from hot to cold. It was bewildering. You never knew what might set him off. Even during their happiest moments, he could suddenly become remote. He could be passionate, demanding, infuriating; he could be generous and occasionally, even kind. But aside from the night after their engagement party, when he'd told her about that horrible woman who'd broken his heart, Santiago had never again let her close. Never let her in.

Thinking about it now, Belle shook her head firmly. There was no point in worrying. Today was her wedding day. She should just relish her joy that Santiago had actually woken up beside her.

Careful not to wake him, she rose quietly from the bed. Going to the bedroom's tall windows, she brushed aside the translucent curtains and looked down at the New York street, which was already starting to stir into life with taxi cabs and pedestrians, in a pale haze of pink and gray.

Tonight after dusk, she and Santiago would be bound together in lifetime vows, surrounded by family and friends. Letty and Darius had come back from Greece with their fat, adorable baby, specifically to attend. Letty would even be coming to the house a few hours early, to help Belle do her hair and makeup for the ceremony. And that wasn't all.

Two days ago, Santiago had sent his private jets to collect Belle's younger brothers: Ray from Atlanta, where he now owned his own plumbing business, and Joe from Denver, where he was training to be a fireman.

Belle had cried when her brothers arrived. It was the first time she'd seen them in two years. For a long time, the three siblings just hugged each other. Her brothers were excited to be uncles. They'd exclaimed both at the size of her belly and the luxurious brownstone mansion.

"You're in a new world now, Belle," Ray had said, pulling off his John Deere cap to survey the foyer in awe. Even their guest rooms had amazed them. Joe confided he was afraid to use the towels, until she'd tartly told him that this was her house and she wouldn't accept any more foolishness. Joe looked at her.

"You're happy, aren't you, Belle?" He shook his head. "I mean, I know this guy's got private jets and mansions and all that. But does he love you? Do you love him?"

And looking at her baby brother's hopeful, pleading face, Belle had done the only thing an older sister could do. She'd lied.

"Of course Santiago loves me." Then she'd realized something horrible. Something that wasn't a lie. She'd whispered, "And I love him."

Two days before her wedding, she'd been forced to face the truth. She was in love with Santiago.

When she'd first accepted his proposal—when he'd blackmailed her into it—Belle had told herself she shouldn't take it personally if Santiago didn't love her. He was just a hard-edged, ruthless tycoon who couldn't love anyone. Love wasn't in his character. She'd told herself she could live with it.

She was wrong.

"I earned a billion-dollar fortune. For her."

She could still hear the raw huskiness of Santiago's voice when he'd told her the story of the woman he'd once loved with all his heart. The night of their engagement party, all her rationalizations had fallen off a cliff.

Santiago did know how to love. Her stomach churned

now as she stared out the window at the waking city. He'd once loved a woman so much he'd spent literally years trying to win her, just like in the fairy tales Belle used to read her brothers when they were little. A peasant boy proves his worth by killing a dragon or vanquishing an army or sailing the seven seas to win the hand of the fair princess.

Only Santiago hadn't won his true love. Instead, the princess had just been one more privilege he was denied because he'd been born the bastard son of a maid. And everything he'd done to prove he didn't care about his father's rejection—from buying the historic ranch in Texas, to building a world-class art collection, to amassing a bigger fortune than him—only proved the opposite.

It doesn't matter, she told herself desperately. It all happened long ago. The woman had married his elder brother and they all lived in Spain, on the other side of the world.

But here in New York, the fairy tale was different. Belle was the peasant, and Santiago the handsome, distant king. She'd have given anything to win him. Slay any dragon, conquer any army. But how?

She might bear his child, but would she ever claim his heart?

Belle looked back at Santiago, still sprawled across their bed. The cool light of dawn was starting to add a soft pink glow through the windows. Her eyes traced the contours and outlines of his muscular, powerful body, with the white sheet twisted around his legs. She longed for him to be hers, really hers.

And in a way, he was. She would be his wife. His partner. His lover.

But never his love.

Going to the en-suite bathroom, she took a long, hot shower, trying to get the anxiety out of her body, and the growing fear of marrying a man she loved, but who would never love her back.

A man who, for all she knew, was still in love with that woman from long ago.

Maybe our baby will bring us together, she tried to tell herself, but she knew this was a delusion. Santiago would be a caring father, and he'd love their daughter. That didn't mean he'd feel anything more than respect for Belle as a partner. Anything more than desire for her in the night.

He would never let her in his heart. He would never slay dragons for her, sacrifice his life for her, as he had for that beautiful Spanish woman long ago.

Getting out of the shower, she wrapped herself in a white fluffy robe. Wiping the steam off the glass, Belle looked at herself in the bathroom mirror. Today was supposed to be the happiest day of her life, but her eyes were suddenly sad.

She looked down at the enormous diamond ring sparkling on her left hand. As ridiculously impractical as it was, as heavy and cold, it was beautiful and special. He'd picked it out just for her. Didn't that mean something, at least?

When she came out into their bedroom, Santiago was gone. He'd told her he would be at the office until shortly before their candlelight ceremony was due to begin, at seven, but she'd somehow hoped he would change his mind and be with her, today of all days. She was desperate for reassurance about their upcoming marriage. She was suddenly terrified she was about to make the biggest mistake of her life, and that she wouldn't be the only one to suffer for it.

Right or wrong, she told herself, the choice has already been made. *I'm marrying him today.*

But the day passed with agonizing slowness, with too much time for her to worry. She saw her brothers at breakfast, right before the two young men set out to see the Statue of Liberty and Empire State Building. She got one last checkup from her obstetrician, then finished last-minute wedding details.

In the late afternoon, it was finally time. She went to her closet and stroked the empire-waist wedding gown of cream-colored lace, tailored to fit her eight-months-plus pregnant belly. She'd found it at a vintage shop in Chinatown, and loved it.

She took a deep breath.

Smoothing rose-scented lotion over her skin, she put on her wedding lingerie, an expensive confection of white satin bralette, panties and white stockings with garter belt. Any moment now, Letty would be here to help with her hair and makeup. Belle would have to somehow pretend to be a blissfully happy bride, hiding how scared she really was that she was doing the wrong thing, permanently giving her life and heart to a man who would never love her back.

I'm marrying him for our daughter, Belle told herself desperately. But would her daughter grow up thinking it was normal for married parents not to love each other? That it was expected and right, to live without love?

Belle felt like she was hyperventilating as she went to the huge closet and took the beautiful wedding dress from the hanger. She heard a hard knock at the door.

Expecting Letty, she called, "Just a sec!"

But the door was flung open. Belle turned with a yelp of protest, trying to hide her half-naked body with the wedding dress. Then she gasped.

"Santiago! What are you doing here? Don't you know it's bad luck to see the bride in her wedding dr—?" Her voice cut off when she saw his face. "What's wrong?"

"My brother…"

"Your brother? Is he here?"

He gave a strangled laugh. "He's dead."

"What?"

His expression was pale and strange. "He died two days ago."

"I'm sorry," Belle whispered. Her wedding dress dropped unheeded to the floor as she went to him. Without thinking, she wrapped her arms around him, offering comfort, not caring that she was wearing only the bra and panties and that it was bad luck. "What happened?"

"Otilio had a heart attack and crashed his car. It's just lucky no one else was hurt."

"I'm so sorry," she repeated, her eyes filling with tears. "Even though you never met, and your relationship was complicated, he was still your brother and..."

"The funeral is tomorrow morning in Madrid."

Belle sucked in her breath. "You'll miss it. You..."

Then he met her eyes, and she suddenly knew.

"You're not going to miss it," she said slowly. "You're going to Madrid."

Santiago gave a single short nod. "I'm leaving immediately."

"But our wedding..." she whispered.

"I've already had my executive assistant start making calls. I'm sorry, Belle. Our wedding must be temporarily put off."

Belle had just been arguing that they were family, but now she said in a small voice, "But you don't even know them."

"My father needs me."

"He called you?"

His jaw tightened. "No. It was my brother's widow who called. She asked me to come, for my father's sake."

"Your brother's..." It took several seconds for this to sink in, and then Belle staggered back a step.

His brother's widow.

His *widow*.

The only woman Santiago had ever loved was free now.

Single.

What must the woman be like, since Santiago had spent years trying to win her love? Beautiful, chic, witty, powerful, sexy, glamorous? All of the above?

How could Belle compare with that?

She couldn't.

She felt sick inside.

"Belle?"

"Um." She tried to gather her thoughts. "It must have been…strange to talk to her again, after all these years."

"It was," he said in a low voice. "She said my father wants to see me. He has no one else now. His wife died years ago. Otilio and Nadia never had any children. I'm the last Zoya."

Belle's lips parted. "Are you saying…?"

"After thirty-five years, the Duque de Sangovia is willing to recognize me as his son."

And with that, Belle suddenly knew that her whole life, and her baby's too, had just changed, because a man she'd never met had had a heart attack in Spain.

"I'm sorry I have to postpone the wedding," he added, but something about his voice made her wonder how sorry he really was. Even as she had the thought, she reproached herself for it. How could she selfishly think about her own hurt, when Santiago's brother had just died, and his father was reaching out to him for the first time?

She put her hand on his arm urgently. "I'll come with you. To Madrid."

He shook his head. "It's across the Atlantic. You're getting too close to your due date to travel."

"I'll manage. I mean—" she gave an awkward laugh "—isn't that why you have a private jet? I just had a checkup this morning and I'm not anywhere close to labor. I'll be fine for a few days."

He looked at her, his jaw tight. "You would be willing

to go to so much trouble, to attend the funeral of a man you've never met? At your state of pregnancy? After I canceled our wedding like this?"

"Of course I would," she said over the lump in her throat. "I'm going to be your wife."

He set his jaw.

"Come, then."

She didn't get the sense that he was overjoyed.

"Unless you don't want me…"

"That's not it. I just don't want you to be uncomfortable."

"I'll be fine. I can't let you face it alone."

"That's very thoughtful." His eyes were unreadable as he looked down at her. "But then, I'd expect no less of you. Such a loving heart."

His words should have cheered her, and yet somehow, they didn't feel like a compliment. They felt like an accusation.

He looked her over in the white silk wedding lingerie, as if not even seeing her. "Change your clothes. Pack as quickly as possible. We leave in ten minutes."

She stared after him, her heart sick with fear.

When she'd woken up that morning, she'd been so scared of marrying Santiago and spending the rest of her life loving him, when he didn't love her back.

But now she realized there could be something even worse than that. Watching as Santiago fell back in love with the beautiful, aristocratic woman who'd once claimed his heart.

CHAPTER EIGHT

MADRID. ROYAL CITY of dreams.

The city was the third largest in Europe, built on a grand scale, from the classical grandeur of the Plaza Mayor to the world-class art of the Prado Museum and designer shops on the wide, graceful Gran Vía.

Santiago hadn't been back to this city since he'd fled at eighteen to make his fortune. Now he was back, no longer a desperate, penniless teenager, but a powerful tycoon, a self-made billionaire.

At fourteen, he'd begged his father to see him. Now the Duque de Sangovia was doing the begging, not him.

Actually, it had been Nadia who'd begged on his father's behalf. It had been strange, unpleasant, to hear her voice on the phone, like resurrecting a long-dead ghost. He'd felt nothing, not even hatred.

Perhaps he should thank her, he thought. She was the one who'd spurred him to become the man he was today. Powerful. Rich.

Heartless.

He stared out the car window as the Duque de Sangovia's chauffeur drove the limousine through the city's clogged morning traffic, carrying Santiago and Belle and their two bodyguards from the private airport. Madrid had once been a medieval dusty village, until King Phillip had moved the royal court here during the Spanish Golden Age. And even back then, the Zoya family had served their king, fighting his battles to build an empire of their own.

Each generation had become more powerful, with a better title to pass on to their heirs. His elder half brother Otilio had been born with the title of *marqués*, raised to be the next duke. But now his brother was dead.

Brother. Such a meaningful word for what had been, in their case, such a nonexistent relationship. Second only to *father*.

Today, at Otilio's funeral, he would finally meet his father in person. All Santiago knew of him came from the news and from his mother's scant stories, when he was very young. And he would see Nadia, the woman he'd once loved, whom he'd thought a kindred spirit. They'd both achieved the dreams they'd had at the orphanage, some twenty years before. He was a billionaire. She was a world-famous actress.

But not a duchess, he thought. That dream, at least, had been lost to her, from the moment her husband died.

He looked out at the weak morning light of Madrid. The September weather was chilly, the sky drizzling rain. He couldn't imagine a more perfect setting for a funeral.

Belle was sitting beside him in the back of the vintage Rolls-Royce limousine, wearing an elegant black shift dress with a long black jacket. It should have been chic, but was somehow ill-fitting and uncomfortable-looking on Belle's pregnant, curvaceous body. She wouldn't meet his eyes.

She'd barely spoken two words to him on the overnight flight across the Atlantic, leaving him alone with his own dark thoughts. She hadn't reproached him about canceling their wedding. Not a single word.

Not one woman in a million would have been so understanding, he thought. But of course Belle was always so kind. So loving.

Emotions were bubbling up inside him, hot as lava. He'd pushed his feelings down for most of his life. He wasn't sure how much longer he could keep it up.

He hadn't gone to his mother's funeral, twenty years before, because there hadn't been one. She'd had no money, the husbands she'd divorced were long gone, and in her frustration and bitterness, she'd alienated most of her friends. Her son was the only one left, and she'd done her best to make him hate her as well, knowing he couldn't leave.

As a young boy, he'd noticed other boys getting hugs and kisses from their mothers, and wondered why Mamá never treated him with such devotion. "Because you're bad all the time," she told him angrily. "You make your stepfathers angry when you don't put away your toys. You make them leave." It had hurt him when he was young. But by the time he was fourteen, he'd realized the real reason she never loved him. She blamed him for all the fairy tales gone wrong. Starting with his father, the duke.

Living in the orphanage, at least he'd known where he stood. He was on his own.

He'd loved New York from the beginning. The city was heartless and cold? Well, so was he. They were perfect for each other.

"Oh, my word," Belle breathed next to him. "Is that the crowd for your brother's funeral?"

Santiago blinked as he saw huge crowds of well-wishers and gawkers standing on the sidewalk outside the cathedral, held back by police. The driver pulled up to the curb, then opened their door.

Santiago got out of the backseat, turning back to assist Belle, who glanced nervously at the crowds, then looked up at him with dark stricken eyes.

Reaching for her hand, he helped her from the limo toward the gothic stone cathedral. The driver held an umbrella over their heads as the rain continued to drizzle from the gray clouds, falling against the vivid yellows and reds of the trees in September.

"It's like all Madrid is here," she whispered. "How famous was he?"

"They're not here for him," he ground out.

Belle frowned. "What do you mean?"

"There's something you should know about his wife…"

But before he could finish, the oversized door of the cathedral opened, and they entered. The nave of the cathedral was crowded with people who'd come to pay their last respects to Otilio, Marqués de Flavilla, the only legitimate son and heir of the powerful Duque de Sangovia, and the husband of the Most Beautiful Woman in the World.

"He died so unexpectedly," he heard someone say sadly as they passed. "Of a heart attack, and at only thirty-six. Such a tragedy to die so young."

"His poor wife…"

"Oh, her. I heard they've been separated for years. She's probably already thinking this will make spectacular PR for her next movie."

Setting his jaw, Santiago walked heavily up the center aisle of the cathedral in his black suit, holding Belle's hand tightly. The crowds parted for them like magic, people whispering around them, their eyes popping out of their heads.

"The duke's secret son…"

"His bastard son…"

"A self-made billionaire from America…"

Everywhere, he saw admiring eyes, curious eyes. All of them, these aristocrats and royals and politicians from around the world, seemed to admire him as he'd once only dreamed of being admired.

Ironic. All it had taken was the death of his brother, and suddenly Santiago had become a Zoya.

His jaw was taut as he came down the aisle, Belle directly behind him. Then he froze.

At the altar, surrounded by flowers, he saw a closed casket covered with a blanket embroidered with the family's coat of arms. The brother he'd never met, the chosen one, the rightful heir. Surrounding the coffin were flowers, tall silver candlesticks and officiants, ponderous in their robes.

Santiago's attention fell on two people in the front row. An old man in a wheelchair. His father. He looked old, compared to the pictures he'd seen. His face looked querulous, and his skin so pale it was almost translucent.

Beside him, patting him on the shoulder, a woman stood in a sleek, short black dress and chic little black hat with netting. Nadia.

At thirty-six, she was tall and thin and blonde, delicate and fragile, like an angel, severely elegant in her dark mascara and red slash of lipstick. He felt the shock of her beauty like the metallic tang of a remembered poison that had once been tasted and nearly been fatal.

Looking up, Nadia's violet eyes pierced him. She lowered her head to whisper to the man in the wheelchair, and the Duque de Sangovia's rheumy eyes abruptly looked up to see Santiago, his thirty-five-year-old bastard son, for the very first time.

For a second, Santiago held his breath. Then he exhaled. What did he care what the man thought of him now?

Behind him, Belle gave a soft, breathy curse that made him turn and stare. She'd never used a curse word in front of him before. Her eyes were wide with horror.

"That's your ex?" she said in a strangled voice. "Nadia *Cruz*?"

"So?" he said shortly.

"So—she's famous! I've seen her movies! She's one of the biggest movie stars in the world!"

"I know," he said impatiently, and strode forward to the end of the aisle, Belle trailing behind him.

"Santiago! Thank the heavens you are here at last," Nadia greeted him in Spanish, anxiously holding out her hands. "Quickly, quickly, it's about to start. We saved you a place…" She drew back with an irritated look as she saw Belle behind him, still clinging to his hand. "Who is this?"

"My fiancée," he responded in the same language. "Belle Langtry."

Belle's hand tightened. She didn't understand Spanish, but she understood her own name.

Nadia gave a smile that didn't reach her eyes and switched to say in clear English, "We only saved one place in the front row. For family only. She'll have to go behind."

"She stays with me," Santiago said automatically, but he was distracted as his father wheeled himself forward.

The Duque de Sangovia was even older than he'd expected. He seemed to have shrunken since last photographed, in the days since his heir had died. He said imperiously to Santiago, "You will sit between Nadia and me." He didn't look at Belle. "Your companion must find another place."

Bereaved or not, Santiago wasn't going to let the old man boss him around. "No, she stays."

But he felt Belle's hand pull away.

"It's fine. I'll get a spot in the back," she said quickly, and disappeared into the crowd. As the choir started to sing, everyone took their seats and Santiago found himself sitting between his father, whose attention he'd once craved so desperately, and the woman he'd once loved so recklessly.

Twisting his head, Santiago saw Belle in her dark black dress and coat sitting three rows behind them. Her lovely face was pale, her dark eyes luminous and sad. Was she so affected by the death of a man she'd never known? But when she met his eyes, she gave him an encouraging smile.

Always so thoughtful. Such a loving heart.

Luring him to trust her. To love her. Luring him to his own destruction.

Santiago turned away, a storm raging inside him.

The priest began the ceremony and he sat numbly, hardly able to feel anything. He barely heard the words as one officiant after another praised his brother, who apparently had been a paragon, beloved by all.

His heart was pounding as he stared at the closed casket, covered with the embroidered Zoya coat of arms and surrounded by flowers, barely hearing the eulogies.

He'd never imagined he would someday be seated beside his father, the duke, in a place of honor, for all the world to see. The old man actually looked at him once or twice during the ceremony, his wizened expression a little bewildered, tears in his eyes.

After the ceremony, they were whisked into the waiting limousine, which had been altered for his father's wheelchair. They were to be taken to the funeral reception at the Zoya *palacio*, a mile away from the cathedral. But as he was led to the limousine behind his father and Nadia, Santiago paused, looking around with a frown.

"Where is Belle?"

"Family only," Nadia told him firmly. He ignored her.

Striding back into the cathedral, he found Belle. "Come with me."

"Where?" She looked uncertain, ill at ease.

"The palace." This time, he wasn't going to let her slip away. Holding her hand tightly, he pulled her into the back of the stretch limousine, where Nadia and his father were already seated.

Belle sat beside him in silence, looking awkward and

uncomfortable and very pregnant, as they faced Nadia and his father, seated opposite. He saw Nadia and the duke both look at the swell of Belle's pregnancy, then look away, as if her condition were a personal affront.

Deafening silence filled the limousine as the driver took them from the cathedral to the Calle de la Princesa. In the middle of Madrid, surrounded by high-rise buildings, was the duke's city residence, the Palacio de las Palmas, with acres of lush greenery behind tall wrought-iron walls and a guarded gate. The same gate from which Santiago had been bloodily barred as an orphaned fourteen-year-old.

They drove past the wide open gate and past the luxurious gardens with the exotic palms for which the neoclassical palace was named. The limo stopped. Santiago's eyes were wide as he saw the nineteenth-century palace for the first time.

But as Santiago started to get out, the duke reached out a shaking claw to his shoulder.

"I thank God you've come to me, boy," he rasped in Spanish. "You are all I have left." He looked at him intently with his hooded gaze. "Truth be told, *mi hijo*, you are the only one who can save this family now."

It had been a very long day, Belle thought wearily. One thing after another. Her interrupted wedding. A private flight across the Atlantic. An elaborate funeral. A palace in Madrid. And oh, yeah, discovering that Santiago's ex was *Nadia Cruz*.

Now this.

Belle felt exhausted and overwhelmed as she looked up at the five-hundred-year-old castle. After the funeral reception had ended in Madrid, they'd traveled ninety minutes to the village of Sangovia, nestled in a valley beneath the castle on the crag, heart of Zoya history and power.

She nearly stumbled over the cobblestones, still slippery with rain in the darkness. Santiago grabbed her arm, steadying her.

He frowned, looking at her. "Are you all right?"

Belle tried to smile encouragingly. "I'm fine."

But she wasn't fine. Not at all. She hadn't been fine since Santiago had canceled their wedding yesterday.

She'd slept fitfully on the private jet over the Atlantic, tossing and turning. Then at the funeral she'd discovered it was even worse than she'd feared.

Santiago's ex, the widowed marquesa, was a famous movie star—famous, beautiful, powerful…everything that she, Belle, was not. And his father, the elderly Duque de Sangovia, had yet to acknowledge Belle's existence, even when he'd been sitting inches away, facing her in the limousine.

After the funeral, at the reception in the Palacio de las Palmas in the center of Madrid, she'd watched as Santiago stood beside his father and Nadia to gravely thank each of the illustrious, powerful guests—prime ministers, presidents, royalty—for coming to honor the late marqués.

Belle stood back, near the tables of food, feeling awkward and alone. The reception lasted for hours, until her belly felt heavy and tight and her feet throbbed with pain. She did not belong here, surrounded by all these wealthy, powerful people, in the gilded palace.

How could she compete with this—any of it?

She'd been intimidated by Santiago's mansion in Manhattan, but the Palacio de las Palmas, with its classical architecture and Greek columns, was an actual palace. There were layers of wealth on every wall, paintings and frescoes on the ceiling and sweeping staircases that led to more gilded rooms with yet more paintings of more illustrious Zoya ancestors.

When the reception finally ended, Belle had breathed a sigh of relief, hoping against hope that Santiago would shake hands with his father and Nadia—or better yet, just wave to the woman from a distance—and he and Belle could get back on a plane for New York.

Instead, Santiago had informed her that he would be remaining in Spain, staying at the castle of Sangovia with his father and Nadia.

"Just until Otilio's will is dealt with."

"Do we have to?"

"You don't. You can go back to New York tonight."

She'd looked up sharply. "No!"

"You are three weeks from your due date," he replied coolly. "You should be home."

He seemed as if he could hardly wait to get rid of her. Once, it would have been a dream come true for her to be sent away. But now, she could hardly bear the thought of it. She'd glared at him. "I'm staying with you."

He ground his teeth. "Belle—"

"We just got to Spain." Her voice trembled, but she lifted her chin. "I'm not going to turn around and fly back to New York. I'm exhausted. I'm staying."

He'd stared at her for a long moment.

"Fine. Stay. Just for a day or two. Then you're going back."

And he hadn't spoken to her again, the whole ninety minutes it took to drive with the duke and the movie star and their bodyguards to the medieval village of Sangovia, tucked in a green valley, beneath the looming castle at the top of the crag.

The castle had looked beautiful from a distance, but as Belle walked through the enormous door, she thought it felt impersonal and cold inside, far worse than the palace in Madrid. The castle of Sangovia wasn't gilded or gleaming like the neoclassical Palacio de las Palmas. The windows were small and far between, and the walls were cold stone. This castle came from an earlier, more brutal time of battles and blood.

The duke said something in Spanish to Santiago, and he replied with a nod. His father disappeared down the cold hallway, past a suit of armor, into a room she couldn't see.

Nadia then said something lightly in the same language, before she too disappeared. For a brief moment, Belle and Santiago were alone in the dark stone hallway. She was suddenly tempted to throw herself in his arms, to ask why he'd been so distant, to try to feel close to him again.

Then they heard a cough, and turning, they saw a uniformed maid. She said in English, "I'm here to take you to your rooms."

"Of course," Santiago said smoothly. "Thank you."

The maid led them through the castle, and up the stairs. A less homey or cozy domicile could scarcely be imagined. It was cold, drafty and damp. The stiff chairs they passed in the hallway all looked hundreds of years old and Belle feared might break if she actually tried to sit on one. Why would anyone choose to live here? she wondered.

The maid led Santiago and Belle to the east wing of the second floor. "All the family's bedrooms are down here," she said shyly, and pushed open a door.

The bedroom was formal and old-fashioned, filled with antiques, including a curtained four-poster bed. Belle glanced out the window at the view of the valley in the twilight.

"What do you think?" Santiago asked in an expressionless voice.

"It's very nice," Belle said politely.

"Thank you," the maid said. She turned to Belle. "I will take you to your room now, *señorita*."

Santiago suddenly scowled. "What are you talking about? My fiancée is staying with me."

"I am sorry, *señor*," the maid replied uncomfortably,

"but His Excellency does not approve of unmarried persons sharing sleeping quarters."

"Oh, really?" Santiago ground out. "Is that why he always used to seduce his maids in closets?"

The woman looked scared. *"Señor—?"*

"Forget it." He gritted his teeth. "You can just tell His Excellency—"

"No, Santiago. It's fine. Really." Belle put her hand on his arm anxiously. "This is his home. He just lost his son. I can sleep in a separate room for a night or two." She gave him a wan smile. "I'm tired. I just want to go to bed."

He started to argue, then scowled at the maid. "Fine. Take us to her room, then."

Rather than looking relieved, the maid looked even more nervous. "His Excellency asked that you come back down immediately to the salon, *señor*. I can take Miss Langtry the rest of the way upstairs."

"Upstairs? How far is it?"

"Um…"

"It doesn't matter," Belle interjected. "Your father needs you. Go to him."

He turned to Belle. "Are you sure?"

"I'm sure."

"I'll check on you later." His expression seemed distant. "And kiss you good night."

Maybe then, she thought hopefully, when they were alone, they could actually talk and try to work out whatever was making him so distant. "All right."

He kissed her gently on the forehead, his lips cool. "Until then."

"This way, *señorita*."

Belle followed the maid down the hall. They went up a sweeping staircase, then a tightly winding flight of steps, then another. Belle's legs started to ache, and once or twice she leaned against the stone wall to catch her breath. The maid seemed to have no trouble whatsoever.

"How many people are on staff here?" Belle asked, to fill the silence as the maid waited.

"Thirty, *señorita*."

"Thirty people work here? To take care of how many?"

"Two."

Reaching a tower, they went up another tightly twisting flight of stairs, this one of rickety wood. Ducking her head, the maid pushed open a door at the back. She sounded embarrassed as she said, "Here is the room assigned to you, *señorita*."

Belle realized they'd put her in the attic, as if she were a mad relative, four floors above Santiago's room in the family wing.

"There's the bathroom," the woman added reluctantly.

Belle peeked past the door to a tiny bathroom, smaller than a closet, with a toilet, bare sink and shower so small she was afraid her belly wouldn't fit. A bare light bulb hung from the ceiling.

The family's opinion of her, and intention for her future, couldn't have been more clear.

"I'm sorry, *señorita*."

Belle forced herself to turn with a bright smile. "No, it's fine."

"You are too kind." The maid added under her breath, "If the marquesa had been assigned to such a room, we would have heard her screaming for miles."

Which was why, Belle reflected, beautiful women like Nadia Cruz ended up with everything they wanted, while girls like Belle ended up in rooms in the attic.

Soon after the maid left, Belle's overnight bag arrived, held by a huffing and puffing porter who glared at her, as if it were her fault he'd been forced to climb so many tightly twisting stone steps. "I'm sorry," she apologized, feeling guilty even though it hadn't been her idea.

Getting on her pajamas, she brushed her teeth and climbed into the tiny single bed, with the sagging mattress and squeaky metal frame, to wait for Santiago.

She looked out through the curtainless small round window. Sweeping moonlight showed all of the tiny village of Sangovia in the valley below the castle. With a shiver, she pulled up the thin blankets around her baby bump, and stared out into the starlit night.

Cuddling her belly, she leaned back against the lumpy pillow, yawning as she tried to stay awake until Santiago came to kiss her good night as he'd promised. She waited. And waited.

But he never came.

CHAPTER NINE

SANTIAGO STARED ACROSS the chilly salon, over a glass of even chillier Scotch, and looked down into his father's eyes, the chilliest of all.

"What are you saying?" His voice sounded strained, even to his own ears.

The old man's reply was a harsh rasp from the bowels of his wheelchair. "You will stay in Spain. As my heir."

Santiago paced a step in the oversized salon, which was filled with Renaissance art and leather-bound books that he'd wager no one had touched in years, except perhaps by the maids dusting them. The two men were alone.

When he'd come downstairs to see his father, the man had wheeled over to the liquor cabinet, poured him a drink, and then spoken his demand without preamble.

Once he would have killed to hear his father say those words. But now...

Santiago took a gulp of Scotch, then said coldly, "You've ignored me for my whole life. Why would I want to be your heir?"

"It is your birthright."

"It wasn't my birthright for the last thirty-five years."

"Everything changed with the death of my son." Suddenly, the old man sounded weary. He ran a hand over his wispy head. "I am dying, Santiago. You are all that is left of the Zoyas now. If you do not take over this family, there will never be another Duque de Sangovia."

Santiago's jaw tightened. "Why should I care? You abandoned my mother. You abandoned me before I was born. What is the dukedom to me? I have my own company. My own empire. My life is not in Spain."

"It could be."

"I came to Otilio's funeral to show my respect, nothing more. And because I was curious to meet the man who never wanted to recognize me as his son."

The elderly Duke said slyly, "And to see Nadia?"

That brought Santiago up short.

The man continued, "She has been a good daughter-in-law to me. She is beautiful, elegant, powerful, famous. The perfect consort." He paused. "Except for her inability to conceive the Zoya heir, but as for that, perhaps it is not too late."

Santiago's eyes narrowed. "What do you mean?"

"I know you and Nadia have a history. Perhaps this is fate. She could still bear the Zoya heir. To you."

Santiago stared down at him, unable to believe what he was hearing. "Have you lost your mind, old man? You've met my fiancée. Belle is upstairs right now. Our baby is due in weeks—"

"You must give that woman up," the Duque de Sangovia said harshly. "She will never be accepted, this country girl, not in Madrid nor in the elite circles of international aristocracy where you belong. It would be cruel to force her into a place where she would always be awkward, rejected, based on her unfortunate background."

"Oh, so you're just looking out for her—is that it?" Santiago said acidly. "You forget I was raised a bastard, without money or formal education—"

"You are different. You are my son, with Zoya blood. You have single-handedly built a business empire that must inspire respect."

In spite of himself, Santiago felt a strange zing of pride

at hearing his father speak those words. Then he caught himself. "So you expect me to abandon her," he ground out, "as you did my mother?"

"*Sí*, and for the same reasons," the duke said calmly. "I could not divorce my wife, the duchess, to run off with a maid. I would have lost all the fortune that came with her, and damaged my family honor and my name."

"Seducing an eighteen-year-old maid and then abandoning your own son is what you call honorable?"

"Sometimes difficult choices must be made. This girl, this Belle, has nothing. She is nothing. Toy with her if you must, even have a child with her, but do not marry her. If you wish to be my heir, you must marry as befits the future Duke of Sangovia."

"I will marry as I choose, and you and Sangovia and Nadia can all go to hell."

"Do not marry this American girl." The old man's rheumy eyes turned hard. "Do you really think she could ever be happy here, in this world? It would be cruel to her. And the child. Let her go."

Santiago opened his mouth to argue. Then he snapped it shut, thinking of the sad, haunted look in Belle's eyes ever since they'd arrived in Madrid.

"Excuse me, Your Excellency." A male nurse appeared at the door. "It is time for your medicine."

The duke nodded grimly. He started to push his wheelchair out of the room, but as he passed Santiago, the duke gripped his arm with a shaking hand.

"You have the power to choose, *mi hijo*. Let the girl go. Accept your birthright as my son. Become my heir, and the future duke, to continue a legacy that has endured for hundreds of years. The dukedom, combined with your vast business empire, plus a marriage to Nadia, would make you one of the most powerful men in the entire world." His beady eyes burned brightly in the shadowy salon. "Think about it."

Santiago was left alone in the salon, with nothing but the glass of Scotch and his own bleak thoughts for company.

His father was offering him everything he'd ever dreamed of as a boy.

A vindication of his worth.

Everything he'd hungered for as a young man.

But that wasn't the only reason he was suddenly tempted. He clawed back his hair.

For the last few months, he'd found himself growing closer to Belle in a way that he'd enjoyed at first, but now terrified him. As their marriage approached, he'd become increasingly on edge. In bed with her, he'd experienced physical joy beyond anything he'd ever imagined. But he'd started to have feelings for her, beyond partnership or even friendship. Against his will, Belle had become too important to him. Her beauty. Her kindness. Her wit. The deep luminosity of her brown eyes.

He found himself drawn to her. *Needing* her.

Like today. Even after he'd made the decision to send her back to New York so he wouldn't worry about her going into labor so far from home, all she'd had to do was raise her poignant gaze to his and ask to stay, and he'd immediately given in. Because he couldn't bear to see her unhappy, not even for a moment.

He didn't like it.

Santiago didn't want to need anyone. He didn't want to be dependent on their happiness for his own peace of mind. Because if you depended on someone—if you cared for them—it left you weak and vulnerable, to be crushed at will by their inevitable betrayal. He'd learned that from childhood. From Nadia.

I know you and Nadia have a history. Perhaps this is fate. She could still bear the Zoya heir. To you.

The thought repelled him. Nadia, for all her angelic beauty, had the soul of a snake. A mercenary, gold-digging snake. The thought of touching her disgusted him.

But at least Nadia would never again tempt him into risking his heart. Not like Belle.

If he was honest with himself, when he'd gotten the call about his brother's death, and realized it gave him the perfect excuse to cancel the wedding—the same wedding he himself had insisted on, demanded, blackmailed Belle into—part of him had been relieved.

Something inside him was afraid of marrying her now. He, who'd never been afraid of anything, was afraid of what would happen if he spoke those vows to Belle, the one woman on earth who held power over him.

Wearily, Santiago left the salon and went up the sweeping stairs toward the second floor. He stopped in front of his own door, suddenly remembering how he'd promised Belle he'd come up and kiss her good night.

He pictured her beautiful face. Her wide, haunting brown eyes, fringed with black lashes. Her full ruby-red lips. Her softness. Her sweetness.

She'd hated him when they'd first met, with good cause. Santiago had pushed people away for most of his life. It wasn't just a game to him; it was necessary for survival. But he'd known from the night he first seduced Belle that she, idealistic and romantic and good-hearted as she was, could be dangerous to his peace of mind. So he'd pushed her away.

That had all changed when he'd found out she was pregnant. He'd forced her into an engagement in Texas. She'd hated him for that.

But Belle didn't hate him anymore. Something had changed in her during their time living in New York. She'd been his hostess. She'd redecorated his home. She'd even traveled with him to Spain when, by rights, she should have slapped his face for canceling their wedding to attend the funeral of a virtual stranger half a world away.

Santiago wanted her. So much. Even picturing Belle now, stretched out on a bed somewhere upstairs, he yearned to see her, hold her, touch her. He'd meant to ask the housekeeper for directions to her bedroom, which he assumed to be even larger and more comfortable than his own, as any pregnant woman deserved. But now…

Hesitating at his own bedroom door, he looked down the dark hallway toward the stairs. His body yearned for the electricity and comfort of her touch. He longed to feel her sweet, hot, lush body naked against his own.

But the cost to his soul was suddenly too high.

Setting his jaw, he turned back to his own bedroom, going inside, closing the door firmly behind him.

He would sleep alone.

Belle woke up alone in the shabby little attic room of the castle, and sat up in a rush. He'd never come up to kiss her last night.

Trying to ignore the hurt, she stretched her muscles, aching from the lumpy mattress. She took a quick, awkward shower in the tiny beat-up bathroom with peeling linoleum, then freshened up, putting on a new dress that, with her full pregnancy, made her look as lumpy as that bed.

Going downstairs, she went to Santiago's bedroom, only to discover it was empty. So were the other bedrooms in the wing. She wandered downstairs, feeling lost, until she found an English-speaking maid who directed her to the breakfast room.

"You should hurry, miss. I'm afraid you're late," she said anxiously.

Late? How could she be late? No one had told Belle anything about breakfast being at any certain time.

She found the formal breakfast room, with its long elegant table, with food spread out on a side table and big arrangements of flowers that made her want to sneeze. When she arrived, Santiago set down his newspaper, his breakfast plate already empty. His dark eyes were cool as, rising from the table, he came forward.

"I missed you last night," she said, staring up at him.

"Sorry. I was busy." He barely looked at her, and kissed her on the cheek as if she were a stranger.

"Did you enjoy sleeping in, Miss Langtry?" cooed Nadia, also rising from the table, looking sexy and chic in a perfectly cut black skirt suit, her light blond hair pulled back into a chignon, a jeweled brooch on her lapel.

"Sleeping in?" Belle stammered.

"We expected you an hour ago."

The duke muttered something darkly in Spanish, but didn't bother to look in Belle's direction, as his servant pushed his wheelchair from the room.

Belle bit her lip as she looked between Santiago and Nadia. "You expected me at a certain time?"

"Breakfast begins strictly at eight," Nadia said sweetly. "As the housekeeper mentioned in your wake-up call this morning."

"I didn't get any—"

"Don't worry." The blonde swept her arm in a generous gesture. "You are a guest, so of course you are free to ignore the rules of our household, no matter how much trouble it might cause everyone. The food has grown cold, so I've instructed the servants to prepare you a fresh breakfast, in addition to their other duties."

"I didn't mean…" Belle stopped when Santiago kissed her forehead. He was dressed in a dark suit. "Are you going somewhere?"

"The lawyer's office," he said. "And to Madrid, to discuss the possibility of donating art to the museum and creating a wing in my brother's name."

"Otilio was an art lover," Nadia purred. Her stiletto heels clicked against the marble floor as she looked up at Santiago with a smile. "Shall we go?"

Oh, *hell* to the no. Belle looked between them. "I'll come with you."

"That's not necessary," Santiago said.

"But I want to."

"It will be very boring for you."

"Please," she implored, holding out her hand.

With visible reluctance, he took it. "As you wish."

She exhaled.

"It's really unnecessary, Miss Langtry," Nadia said. She looked seriously annoyed.

Belle was glad. The other woman might be in charge in this castle, arranging to exile her to the attic room and sabotaging her in front of Santiago and the household, but Belle wouldn't give up Santiago without a fight.

But, it seemed, neither would Nadia. Later that morning, as the duke and Santiago were in the adjoining office, speaking to the lawyers, the two women sat together in the posh waiting room.

Bright sunlight was pouring through the windows, and cushy chairs lined the walls. The sound of secretaries typing on keyboards came from the next room. Sitting across from Nadia, Belle felt nervous and awkward and tried to hide it by reading a magazine. In Spanish. Upside down.

"How charming," Nadia said suddenly.

Sheepishly, Belle turned around her magazine. But the other woman wasn't looking at her reading material. Reaching out, she touched the diamond on Belle's finger.

"Oh, the ring?" Belle smiled. "Yes, I love it. His proposal was very romantic, too." Maybe it was stretching the truth to call the way he'd blackmailed her into marriage in Texas romantic, but she hated the smirk on the movie star's face.

"Was it?" Nadia smiled back. "I mean, I know it's very *au courant* to recycle these days, but this is taking it a bit far, don't you think?"

"What do you mean?" Belle said stiffly. She guessed from the context that *au courant* meant trendy, though for all she knew it could have been a type of jam.

"Oh, didn't you know?" The blonde's smile widened. "That's the same ring Santiago once used to propose to me."

Belle's heart fell to the wooden parquet floor.

"No," she stammered. "You're mistaken. He picked it out just for me."

"Oh, didn't he tell you? That naughty creature." Nadia's smile turned wicked. "He tried to give it to me five years ago. Regrettably, he'd waited too long and I'd already been spoken for. But I know my diamonds."

Belle wrapped her hand around the ring, feeling completely betrayed. But she couldn't show it, couldn't let the other woman see how her barb had found its target. She tried to shrug. "Even if it's the same ring, we have a totally different situation. I never betrayed him."

"No, you just got pregnant."

Belle's eyes narrowed. "While you made him chase you all those years, then married his brother."

Nadia looked at her with a taunting smile on her red lips. "I'm not married to him anymore. Now I am free."

Belle stiffened, trying to hide her growing fear. "You think you can take him from me."

Nadia tilted her head, considering. "You're not so stupid after all."

Belle's cheeks flushed. "You don't deserve to be Santiago's wife."

"I'm more deserving than you."

"I love him."

"That I can easily believe." The movie star's famous violet eyes cut through her. "But does he love you?"

The burn on Belle's cheeks intensified.

Because that was the heart of it. Santiago didn't love her. He never had. He never would.

That was the truth she'd been fighting to deny, to hide, even from herself. Even though he'd once told her to her face that he would never love her, she'd dreamed he might change.

She mumbled, "He proposed to me…"

"He proposed to me first. With that exact ring." Nadia gave her a hard smile. "Curious, don't you think, that he kept it all these years?"

Belle tried to fight the emotions swirling inside her beneath the other woman's hard gaze. "He was the one who demanded marriage when he found out I was pregnant…"

"And he obviously felt strongly about it, since he couldn't even be bothered to get you your own ring." Nadia leaned forward in her chair, smiling pleasantly. "The ring was mine. As his love was mine. And both will be again."

Belle couldn't breathe. Her heart was pounding frantically. "You're wrong…he won't…"

"No?" Grabbing her arm, Nadia said, "I am Santiago's equal as you never were. We are meant to be together."

Each word hurt more than the last. "You gave him up," Belle choked out, struggling to pull her arm away.

"I had to be ruthless to get what I wanted. Santiago of all people will understand this, and respect it." Her red lips lifted in a smile. "He's loved me since we were teenagers. He's ached for me. Hungered for me. We belong together. My choice to marry his brother only made Santiago want me more." She looked Belle over contemptuously. "Do you really think he would ever choose you, now I'm free?"

No, she didn't. That was what hurt the most.

"There are two ways to do this," Nadia said sweetly. "Either give Santiago up gracefully. Or watch helplessly as I take him from you."

"You can't…"

"If you love him like you say you do, at least leave him thinking of you with some respect."

Pain ripped through Belle. She felt her baby kick inside her as if her daughter was angry, too. She put her hands over her belly. "He's the father of my child."

"After we are wed, I will give him another baby. He will forget yours." Nadia smiled. "Santiago is an honorable man. He will always provide for you and your child, as a matter of duty. You will never have to work again. Consider yourself lucky. Leave Spain. Go seek the love that Santiago will never give you."

Belle swallowed, her heart pounding.

As the door to the lawyer's office opened and the men came out, Nadia whispered, "End it quickly, and it will be better for everyone. Especially you."

With a final friendly pat to Belle's shoulder, Nadia rose to her feet with a beaming smile to greet the duke and Santiago, who was pushing his father's wheelchair.

"Are you boys finally done? Because we are due at the museum." She added teasingly, with her violet-blue eyes flashing between the duke and Santiago, "You men always like to talk and talk…"

Numbly, Belle pushed herself up from the chair. No one was paying attention to her. The three others were talking in Spanish as they walked ahead of her out of the lawyer's office.

In the limo, she sat silently beside Santiago as they traveled through the sun-drenched streets of Madrid. He gave her a curious glance.

But this time, she was the one avoiding his gaze.

"He's loved me since we were teenagers. He's ached for me. Hungered for me. We belong together."

Belle swallowed over the ache in her throat as she watched the passing city through the car window. She'd only met Santiago a year ago. He'd never loved her. And what did they even have in common, when she barely knew the name of her great-grandparents, compared with Santiago, who had an aristocratic bloodline that went back to the Middle Ages?

"After we are wed I will give him another baby. He will forget yours."

Belle knew Santiago's determination to uphold his honor and give their unborn daughter a better childhood than he himself had had. He would not abandon his promise to marry Belle.

She shivered as they traveled in luxury, in a limousine through the streets of Madrid.

The real question was, could she actually let him keep his word, and marry her, trapping them both forever in a cold marriage without love?

CHAPTER TEN

SANTIAGO GLANCED AT the duke as they drove through Madrid. His father had actually thanked him for helping deal with some legal business at the lawyer's office, some contracts that Otilio hadn't signed properly.

His father. It was strange thinking of the old man that way. For the first time, he had a real, flesh-and-blood father.

The old man wasn't affectionate, or even kind. He was arrogant and controlling, and seemed to think that he could boss Santiago around, using his inheritance as bait. Just look at his ridiculous demand that Santiago betray his promise to wed Belle…

He glanced at her now, sitting quietly beside him in the backseat, biting her lip as she stared out at the city streets. She'd been strangely quiet since they'd left the lawyer's office. It wasn't like her to be so quiet. Usually she couldn't wait to tell him exactly what she was thinking, particularly when it insulted him.

No, Santiago suddenly realized. That wasn't true anymore. She didn't insult him anymore, not like she used to. Now, she treated him with encouragement. With…love?

The limo bounced over a bump in the road, and his shoe hit the stiletto across from him. He looked up at Nadia, who was sitting across from him, beside his father. She lifted her dark lashes and smiled.

His father obviously wasn't the only one who believed he could get power over Santiago.

It made him incredulous. How could Nadia not realize he had nothing but contempt for her?

Both she and his father were trying to buy him. They offered him a dukedom like a prize, and thought they could use words like honor and fate, and welcome him into the castle, and Santiago would be grateful. They thought he'd never grown up from the childhood dream he'd had as a lonely, fatherless boy. They thought that all they had to do was offer and Santiago, a self-made independent billionaire, would instantly become an obedient son to the father who'd abandoned him, a grateful husband to the woman who'd betrayed him.

But Santiago Velazquez was no man's pawn—or woman's. His jaw tightened as he looked from Nadia to Belle, who was still staring out the window as if her life depended on it. He was just grateful that she had no idea what his father had proposed. He didn't want her hurt. Especially since…

As his gaze traced over her full rosy lips and the plump curves of her body, something twisted in his heart.

Belle was a woman like no other. Her loyalty and courage and honesty didn't just inspire respect, but reverence. She drew him in. He wanted to let her love him.

He wanted to love her back.

His heart was suddenly pounding.

No.

He couldn't be that stupid.

No one could be as honest, or loyal, or good as he thought Belle was. However she might seem. If he let her inside his heart, he would regret it.

When they reached the famous art museum in the heart of Madrid, he got out quickly, opening his passenger door before the driver could. Belle, too, stepped out quickly, as if she were afraid he might offer his hand to help her out.

At least they were in agreement on one thing right now, he thought grimly. Avoiding each other.

They were parked on the quiet side of the museum, far from the long queues of tourists. He pushed his father's wheelchair toward the side door, which led to the museum's administrative offices. Nadia walked beside the duke, chattering to him charmingly in Spanish. Belle walked silently behind, with the bodyguards and his father's nurse, as if she preferred to be with the staff, rather than with the aristocrats.

She probably did, Santiago thought.

Castilian-accented Spanish whirled around him as they were escorted into the lobby and whisked into the director's office, where they were offered champagne or coffee. Through it all, Belle held herself back from the others, looking miserable and wan and as if her feet hurt.

Becoming a duchess in Spain, traveling with the jet-set, would require more rules that Belle wouldn't like, Santiago thought. He would have to live by new rules as well, but at least he spoke Spanish. At least he was of Spanish blood. Belle wasn't.

Plus, she'd have to temper her honest, enthusiastic, joyful nature to be cool and calm, to know how to smile pleasantly while speaking cutting words, to maneuver the hard merciless edges of the highest of European high society— a world of not just mere money, but hundreds of years of history and breeding, of jostling for position.

Santiago knew he could win in that world, if he chose, because of both his heritage and his personal ruthlessness. He'd spent twenty years fighting in business, tearing other men's companies apart. He knew how to battle. He wasn't afraid of war. He had a thick skin and sharp weapons.

Belle was different. She wasn't a gold digger; she wasn't

a social climber. She'd barely seemed to tolerate New York City. He suspected she'd be happier just tending flowers in their garden, baking for their children, volunteering at their school and caring for her neighbors. She would be happy to be with a man who appreciated her every day when he hugged his family in a warm, loving home. A man who would fix things around the house. Who'd sit on the floor with their young daughter and patiently have a tea party with her dolls.

Belle didn't want to marry a powerful billionaire, or a sexy playboy, or a famous duke. What she really wanted— what she *needed*—was a good man who would love her.

His father's hoarse words came back to haunt him.

"Do you really think she could ever be happy here, in this world? It would be cruel to her. And the child. Let her go."

Belle climbed wearily up the last flight of stairs to her bedroom in the top tower of the castle, then fell exhausted into her small bed.

After the day she'd had, watching Santiago and Nadia and the Duque de Sangovia be fêted and honored in Spanish while she was shunted and ignored, she felt weary to the bone. To the heart.

They'd finally arrived back at the castle, and the others had gone for a drink in the salon. She'd come upstairs for a nap. She barely felt the late afternoon sunlight from the tiny round window warm her skin, and she fell asleep.

When she woke, the room was shadowy and gray, and she saw Santiago's handsome face above her, his jaw tight, his eyes hard.

"This is your bedroom? This—closet?"

She was startled, still half lost in the sensual, heart-breaking dream she'd been having about him. "What are you doing up here? What's wrong?"

"I came to get you for dinner. Nadia never sends any-one to tell you, does she?"

"No," she said frankly. "She wants you for herself."

His startled eyes met hers. "You know?"

"Of course I know. But she can't have you." Belle put her hand on his sculpted cheek, rough with a five-o'clock shadow. Something suddenly gave her courage. Maybe it was this moment of intimacy, of honesty. Maybe it was because, just a moment ago, she'd been dreaming of him making love to her. But looking him straight in the eye, she whispered, "Because I love you, Santiago…"

For a moment, she trembled with terror that she'd ad-mitted it. She couldn't meet his eyes, so leaning up, she kissed him, full on the mouth. It was the first time she'd ever initiated a kiss, and she embraced him with all her pent-up hunger and desperate love.

And in the tiny single bed, tucked by the attic win-dow, a miracle happened—Santiago gripped her shoulders tightly and kissed her back even more desperately than she'd kissed him. He held her as if he were drowning, and Belle was his only chance of saving himself. Exhilaration flooded through her body. She pulled away.

"I love you," she repeated joyfully, searching his dark gaze. "Could you ever love me?"

But when he looked down at her, his handsome face was suddenly cold.

"I never asked for your love, Belle. I never wanted it."

She sucked in her breath, annihilated by pain. How could he kiss her so desperately one moment, then push her away so coldly the next?

Then suddenly it all made sense.

The coldness. The distance. It had all started weeks ago.

He wasn't a fool. He must have realized she was fall-ing in love with him, probably before she even realized it herself. So he'd started pulling away, acting cold. He must have started regretting his decision to propose. When he'd first heard the news of his brother's death—that was why he'd seemed almost relieved to have the excuse to cancel their wedding.

He didn't want her love.

Her shoulders fell. "You told me from the beginning that you'd never love me." Her voice was low. "But I fell for you anyway. For the man you are and the man you could be. I couldn't stop myself from loving you…"

Santiago gripped her shoulders. "Stop saying that." Taking her hand, he pulled her from the bed. "We'll discuss this later. We should go down to dinner. They're waiting for us."

He didn't look at her as they went down the twisting wooden staircase, and all the stairs after that, to the great hall.

Belle's throat ached with unshed tears as they reached the enormous room, two stories high, with paintings that looked hundreds of years old. At the center of the room was a long table that could have easily fit thirty people, but tonight had only two at the end: the elderly duke, who as usual didn't acknowledge Belle's existence, and Nadia, who as usual looked wickedly sexy and beautiful.

Behind her on the wall was an old portrait of a beautiful woman in a black mantilla and elaborate gown, with expressive eyes and a hard smile. Just like Nadia's.

Who was the obviously correct consort for Santiago now? Belle, with her average looks and former job as a waitress, a regular girl from small-town Texas? Or Nadia, an international movie star, the most beautiful woman in the world, who knew how to smile sweetly as she cut you to the heart—the woman Santiago had once loved so much that he'd literally earned a billion dollars to try to win her?

The duke muttered something in Spanish beneath his breath.

Looking up, Nadia said to Belle, "Late again? Honestly, you don't look like the kind of girl who's always late to meals."

Belle growled under her breath, but to her surprise, Santiago answered for her. "Thanks to you."

Nadia tilted her head innocently. "I don't know what you mean."

"You know perfectly well. Sticking Belle up in the tower. You've been doing your best to sabotage her. Stop it," he said sharply, then his voice turned gentle as he said to Belle, "Sit here. Beside me."

A moment later, Belle was eating dinner without much appetite, and drinking water as the others drank red wine and spoke in Spanish. She'd just told her future husband she loved him, and nothing had happened. Wasn't courage supposed to be rewarded in life?

But she didn't think it would be.

She ate numbly, then rose to her feet to escape the dreary, formal table. Santiago stopped her with a glance and four quiet words.

"We need to talk."

And looking at him, Belle was suddenly afraid.

He led her outside, to the Moorish garden behind the castle courtyard. She could see the lights of the castle above and the village below. A few lampposts dotted through the palm trees and fountains of the dark-shadowed garden. Moonlight silvered the dark valley.

Folding his arms, Santiago stood over her, handsome as a fierce medieval king. "Take back your words."

"I can't." She felt like she was going to faint. It was one thing for her to think of leaving him, but something different if he told her to go. Much more final.

His forehead furrowed as he came closer. He was

dressed in a sleek suit, his dark hair cut short. She missed the rougher man she remembered in New York. The one who could laugh, whose hair was a little more wild, especially when he raked it impatiently with his hands. "You don't even like it here."

"Because I don't belong here," she said quietly. "But neither do you."

For a long moment, he looked at her. She saw the clench of his jaw in the moonlight. When he spoke, his voice was hard.

"I'm sending you back to New York."

"You're staying?"

"Yes."

"And you're glad." She choked out a laugh, wiping tears that burned her. "Right. I get it. Let's face it, I was always your second-choice bride. You never really wanted to marry me. You just wanted to do the right thing for our baby."

"I still do," he said quietly. "But as I told you from the beginning, love was never supposed to be part of it."

Her honesty had ruined any chance they had, she realized. When she'd told him she loved him—that had been the thing that had made him finally decide to end this.

"I'm sorry," he said quietly.

She tried to smile, but couldn't. Her cheeks wouldn't lift. She turned away.

Suddenly, she just wanted this to be over as soon as possible. She pulled off her diamond ring, tugging it hard to get it off her pregnancy-swollen finger. Afraid to touch him—afraid if she did, she would cling to him, sob, slide down his body to the ground and grip his leg as she begged him never to let her go—she held it out. "Here."

He stared at the ring without moving to take it. Why was he trying to make her suffer? Why wouldn't he just take it? She slid it into his jacket pocket. She again tried to smile, and again failed. "The ring was never really mine, anyway. You bought it for her."

Santiago stared at her. "She told you?"

"At the lawyer's office." With a choked laugh, Belle looked up at the castle towers overhead. "You know, every time I hear the tap-tap-tap of her stiletto heels, I've started to feel like a swimmer seeing a shark fin in the water." Lifting her gaze to his, she took a deep breath and forced herself to say simply, "But she's like you. You've known her half your life. I can see why you love her."

"Love her?" He sounded shocked. "Don't be ridiculous. She's my brother's widow. He's not even cold in his grave."

Why was he trying to deny what was so plain, even to her? "And now she's free. The only woman you ever loved. The woman you spent years trying to deserve, like a knight on a charger, determined to slay dragons for her. Just like in a fairy tale." She looked up. "And now you'll be duke and duchess. You'll live in a castle in Spain." She looked up at the moonlit castle in wonder, then down at herself as she stood in the garden, heavily pregnant and with ill-fitting, wrinkled clothes, and whispered, "I'm no man's prize."

Reaching out, he cupped her cheek. "It's better for you, Belle," he said quietly. "I can't give you the love you deserve. Now, you'll have a chance at real happiness."

She felt frozen, heartsick. "And our baby?"

"We will do as you suggested in Texas, and share custody. Neither you nor our daughter will ever want for anything. You will always have more money than you can spend. I will buy you a house in New York. Any house you desire."

A lump rose in her throat. "There's only one house I want," she whispered. "*Our* house. The one I decorated, with our baby's first nursery. With Anna and Dinah. Our house, Santiago."

He looked down at her. "I'm sorry."

She looked down at her bare left hand. Once she left him, she thought, all his childhood dreams could come true. He would be a true Zoya. He'd have his father. His position as heir. The woman he'd once loved.

Life was short. Love was all that mattered.

She had to accept it. To set him free, and herself free as well.

Weak with grief, Belle looked up at him. And with a deep breath, she forced herself to say the words that betrayed her very soul. "I'll leave you, then. Tomorrow."

"Tonight would be better. I'll call my pilot and order the plane ready."

Santiago's voice was so matter-of-fact, so cold. As if he didn't care at all. While her own heart was in agony. She wanted to cry. Her voice trembled. "You're in such a rush to get rid of me?"

His jaw set. "Once the decision is made, it's best to get it over with. You deserve better than me. A good man who can actually love you back."

"You could be that man," she whispered. She struggled to smile, to find a trace of her old spirit, even as her eyes were wet with tears. "I know you could."

Emotion flashed across his handsome face, but before she could identify it, it was gone. He looked away.

"I am doing the best I can," he said in a low voice. "By letting you go."

It was a civilized ending to their engagement. They could both go forward as partners raising their baby, telling friends that the breakup had been "mutual" and their engagement had ended "amicably."

But Belle couldn't end it like that.

She couldn't just leave quietly, with dignity. Her heart

rebelled. She couldn't hold back her real feelings. Not anymore.

"I know I can't compete with Nadia," she choked out, "not in a million years. I'm not beautiful like her. I can't offer you the dukedom you've craved all your life. There's only one thing I can give you better than anyone else. My love. Love that will last for the rest of my life." She looked up at him through her tears. "Choose me, Santiago," she whispered. "Love me."

For a moment, blood rushed in her ears. She felt like she was going to faint in the moonlit garden. The image of the looming castle swirled above her. She swayed on her feet, holding her breath.

Then she saw his answer, by the grim tightening of his jaw.

"That's why I'm ending this, Belle," he said in a low, rough voice. "I care for you too much to let you stay and waste your life—your light—on me."

The brief hope in her heart died. Her shoulders sagged. "All right," she said, feeling like she'd aged fifty years. "I'll go pack."

But as she started to turn, he grabbed her wrist. "Unless…"

"Unless?" she breathed.

"You tell me you don't love me after all. Tell me you were lying. We could still be married, like we planned. If you don't ask for more than I can give."

He was willing to still marry her?

For a moment, desperate hope pounded through her.

Then she went still.

Seven years ago, when Justin had first proposed to her, she'd known even then, deep down, that he didn't love her. When he'd demanded Belle have the medical procedure to permanently prevent pregnancy—a monstrous demand, when she'd been only a twenty-one-year-old virgin—barely more than a kid herself—Belle had deluded herself into thinking she had to accept any sacrifice as the price of her love for him.

No longer. She looked up at Santiago in the moonlit garden.

"No," she said quietly.

He looked incredulous. "No?"

Belle lifted her chin. "I might not be a movie star, I might not have a title or fortune, but I've realized I'm worth something too. Just as I am." She took a deep breath. "I want to be loved. And I will be, someday." She gave him a wistful smile. "I just wish it could have been by you."

"Belle…"

Her belly suddenly became taut. Her lower back was hurting. She was still weeks from her due date so she knew it couldn't be labor. It was her body reacting, she thought, to her heart breaking.

"I will always love you, Santiago," she whispered. Tears spilled down her cheeks as she reached up to cradle his rough chin with her hand one last time. "And think that we could have been happy together. Really happy."

Standing on her tiptoes, she kissed one cheek, then the other, then finally his lips. She kissed him truly, tenderly, with all her love, to try to keep this last memory of him locked forever in her heart.

Then, with desperate grief, she pulled away at last.

"Goodbye," she choked, and fled into the castle, blinded by tears. She went up to her room in the tower and packed quickly. It was easy, since she left all of the expensive, uncomfortable new clothes behind. When she came downstairs, she saw a limo in the courtyard waiting for her.

"I'll take your bag, miss," the driver said.

Belle climbed in to the limo, looking back at the castle one last time. She had a glimpse of Santiago in the library window, alone in the cold castle, the future Duke of Sangovia, the future husband of a *marquesa*, a self-made billionaire, sleek and handsome with cold, dead eyes staring after her.

Then, like a dream, he was gone.

CHAPTER ELEVEN

SANTIAGO STOOD AT the library window, watching Belle's limo disappear into the dark night. He felt sick at heart. It was the hardest thing he'd ever done, letting her go.

"Finally. She's gone."

Nadia's voice was a purr behind him. Furious, Santiago turned to face her with a glare. She smiled at him, with a hand on her tilted hip, in front of the dark wood paneling and wall of old leather-bound books. She looked like a spoiled Persian cat, he thought irritably. He bared his teeth into a smile.

"You did your part to get rid of her, didn't you? Sticking her in the tower, undercutting her with the staff, telling her the engagement ring had once been yours?"

"She didn't belong here," she said lazily. "Better for her to just go."

Yes, Santiago thought dully. It would be better. That was the only reason he'd let Belle go. He couldn't bear to be loved by her, and she refused to marry him without it.

Belle, of all women on earth, deserved to be happy. She deserved to be loved.

The truth was, he had no idea what she'd seen to love in him. He'd taken her from her Texas hometown against her will, and yet she hadn't just gone back with him to New York: she'd done her best to fit into his life and play the role of society wife. He remembered how scared she'd been, but she'd done it anyway. Because he'd asked her to.

She'd redecorated his Upper East Side mansion, turning it from a cold showplace to a warm, cozy home. She'd reorganized his staff, removing the arrogant butler, making the household happier.

Belle had been unbelievably understanding when he'd canceled their wedding hours before the ceremony. She'd even insisted on coming to Spain with him.

"I can't let you face it alone," she'd told him.

But now he was alone, in this cold place.

"It was unpleasant, having her always hovering around us. Such a pushy girl," Nadia said, then gave him a bright smile. "Your father sent me to find you. He wants to discuss how soon you might take over the family's business interests." She gave a hard laugh. "You'll do better than Otilio did, that's for sure."

Santiago turned to her abruptly. "Did you love my brother?"

She blinked. *"Love* him?"

"Did you?"

Nadia laughed mirthlessly. "Otilio spent most of his time getting drunk and chasing one-night stands. You heard he died from a heart attack?"

"Yes…"

She shook her head. "He was drunk, and crashed his car into the window of a children's charity shop. It was night and the shop was empty, or else he might have taken out a bunch of mothers and their babies, too. That would have been awful…for our family's reputation." She sighed. "But he wanted a beautiful, famous wife, and I wanted a title. We were partners, promoting the brand of our marriage." She shrugged. "We tried not to spend too much time together."

Partners, Santiago thought dully. Just like he'd suggested to Belle. As if it would be remotely appealing to anyone with a beating heart to accept marriage as a business arrangement, as a brand, as a cheap imitation for what was supposed to be the main relationship of one's life.

He could hardly blame her for refusing.

I love you, Belle had whispered in the shadowy light of that threadbare little attic room. *Could you ever love me?*

And he, who was afraid of nothing, had been afraid.

Santiago told himself that he was glad Belle was gone, so he didn't have to see her big eyes tugging at his heart, pulling him to…what?

"The duke wants you to be on a conference call regarding the Cebela merger."

"Right." He hadn't been listening. He followed Nadia out of the library toward his father's study, feeling numb. He liked feeling numb. It was easy. It was safe.

But late that night, he tossed and turned, imagining Belle on his private jet, flying alone across the dark ocean. What if the plane crashed? And she was so close to her due date. What if she went into labor on the plane? Why hadn't he sent a doctor with her?

Because he'd been so eager to get her away from him.

Not eager. Desperate.

"I love you. Could you ever love me?"

When Santiago finally rose at dawn, he felt bleary-eyed, more exhausted than he'd been the night before. It was the middle of the night in New York, but he didn't care. He phoned the pilot. The man politely let him know that they'd arrived safely in New York, and Miss Langtry had been picked up at the airport by his usual driver and the bodyguard.

"Is there a problem?" the pilot asked.

"No problem," Santiago said abruptly and hung up.

He pushed down his emotions, determined to stay numb. He went downstairs in the castle and ate breakfast, reading newspapers, just as Nadia and his father did. Three people silently reading newspapers at a long table in an elegant room filled with flowers, the only sound the rustle of paper and the metallic clank of silverware against china.

Santiago went numbly through the motions of the day, speaking to his father's lawyers, skipping lunch for a long conference call with a Tokyo firm in the process of being sold to Santiago's New York-based conglomerate.

He didn't contact Belle. He tried not to think about her. He was careful not to feel, or let himself think about anything deeper than business. He felt utterly alone. Correction: he didn't feel anything at all.

Exactly as he'd wanted.

At dinner that night in the great hall, both his father and his sister-in-law were lavish in their abuse of the woman who'd left them the previous night.

"Nothing but a gold digger," Nadia said with a smirk. "As soon as I told her you'd always support the baby she left, didn't she?"

Santiago stared at his crystal goblet with the red wine. Red, like blood, which he no longer could feel beating through his heart.

"You did the right thing, *mi hijo*," the old man cackled, then started talking about a potential business acquisition. "But these money-grubbing peasants refuse to sell. Do they not know their place? They refused my generous offer!" He drank more wine. "So we'll just take the company. Have our lawyers send a letter, say we already own the technology. Check the status of the patents. We can ruin him then take his company for almost nothing."

"Clever," Nadia said approvingly.

Santiago didn't say anything. He just stared down at his plate, at the elegant china edged with twenty-four-carat gold. At the solid silver knife beside it. He took a drink of the cool water, closing his eyes.

All he could think of was Belle, who'd tried to save him

from the cold reality of his world. From the cold reality of who he'd become, as dead as the steak on this plate.

Belle had tried to be his sunshine, his warmth, his light. She'd loved him. And for that, he'd sent her away forever. Both her and his unborn daughter.

"You are very quiet, *mi hijo*."

"I'm not very hungry. Excuse me," Santiago muttered and left the dinner table with a noisy scrape of his hard wooden chair. In the darkened hallway, he leaned back against the oak-paneled wall and took a deep breath, trying to contain the acid-like feeling in his chest. In his heart.

Tomorrow, his father intended to hold a press conference to announce that Santiago would be taking the Zoya name as rightfully his, along with the Zoya companies, eventually folding his own companies into the conglomerate. The duke also would start the process of getting Santiago recognized as the heir to his dukedom.

He was going to be the rightful heir, as he'd dreamed of all his life. He was about to have everything he'd ever wanted. Everything he'd ever dreamed of.

And he'd never felt so miserable.

If he closed his eyes in the hallway, he could almost imagine he could smell the light scent of Belle's fragrance, tangerine and soap and sunshine.

Suddenly, he had to know she was doing all right. It was early afternoon in New York. Reaching for his phone, he dialed the number of the kitchen in his Upper East Side mansion.

Mrs. Green answered. "Velazquez residence."

"Hello, Mrs. Green," Santiago said tightly. "I was just wondering if my wife—" Then he remembered Belle was not his wife, not even his fiancée, and never would be again. He cleared his throat. "Please don't disturb Belle. I just wanted to make sure she is doing well after her trip home."

There was a long pause. Her voice sounded half surprised, half sad. "Mr. Velazquez, I thought you knew."

"Knew what?"

"Miss Langtry is at the hospital... She's in labor."

He gripped the phone. "But it's too soon—"

"The doctors are concerned. Didn't she call you?"

No, of course Belle hadn't. Why would she now, when he'd made it so clear he wanted nothing to do with her? Or their baby girl?

"Thank you, Mrs. Green," he said quietly and hung up. He felt sick, dizzy.

"Something wrong?"

Nadia found him in the hallway. He didn't like having her so close, blocking the sunshine and soap with her heavy smell of exotic flowers and musk.

She frowned, looking at the phone still clasped tightly in his hand. "Bad news?"

"Belle's in the hospital."

"She was hurt?"

"She's gone into labor early."

Nadia shrugged. "Maybe things will go badly. Otherwise you're on the hook for the next eighteen years. If you're lucky, they'll both conveniently die and... Stop, you're hurting me!" she suddenly cried.

Looking down, Santiago saw he'd grabbed her by the shoulder in fury, and his fingers were digging into her skin. He abruptly let her go. The skin on his hand still crawled from touching her.

"You are a snake."

Rubbing her shoulder, she said, "We both are. That's why we're perfect for each other."

He ground his teeth. "My brother is barely in his grave."

"It was always you I wanted, Santiago."

"You had a funny way of showing it."

Nadia shrugged, smiling, still certain of her charm.

"I had to be practical, darling. I didn't know then that you would turn out to be worth so much." She tilted her head, fluttering her long eyelashes. "And what can I say? I wanted to be a duchess."

His lip curled. "You disgust me."

Nadia frowned in confusion. "Then why did you send that girl away? Wait. Oh, no." Her lips spread in a shark-like smile. "You *love* her," she taunted. "Sweet, true, *tender* love."

His voice was tight. "I don't."

"You do. And that baby as well. You wanted to kill me just now, for speaking as I did. You love them both."

Santiago stared down blindly at Nadia in the castle hallway.

Love Belle?

Love her?

He'd let her go because it was better for her. That was all. Because she deserved to be happy. And because his family needed him here in Spain.

But he suddenly realized that wasn't the *whole* reason.

For months now, he'd been fighting his feelings for Belle. Because since he was a boy, every time he'd loved someone, they'd stabbed him in the back. He'd vowed to never play the sucker again.

But with Belle, he'd been tempted more than he could resist. He'd come to care about her too much. He'd started feeling that her happiness was more important than his own.

He hadn't sent Belle away so he could be with his family, but because he was fleeing from them.

Belle was his real family. Belle and the baby.

And that fact terrified him.

Santiago's knees trembled beneath him. He felt a wave rip through his soul, cracking it open.

He'd let her go because he was afraid. Afraid of being

vulnerable. Afraid of getting hurt. Afraid of what would happen, who he would become, if he let her love him.

If he loved her back.

"So it's really true." Nadia looked stunned. Her violet eyes narrowed with rage. "You'd choose that little nobody over me?"

Santiago thought of Belle's many joys, her tart honesty, her silliness, her kindness. He thought of her luminous eyes and trembling pink lips as she'd whispered, *"There's only one thing I can give you better than anyone else. My love."*

For the first time, he saw the truth.

When he was a boy, he'd dreamed of being loved by his father, who was rich and powerful and able to command people from a palace. He'd thought if he could just get the duke to call him son, he'd be happy.

As a young man, he'd dreamed of being loved by Nadia, with all her cold beauty and utter lack of pity. He'd thought he'd be happy if he could just win her. Like a trophy.

But today, at thirty-five, he suddenly realized happiness had nothing to do with that kind of so-called love. Wealth and power, physical beauty, what did they have to do with love? Those things didn't last.

Real love did.

Love was having the loyalty and devotion of a kind-hearted, honest woman. A woman who could make you laugh. Who always had your back. Who would protect and adore you through good times and bad. Who cared for your child. A woman who was the heart of your home. The heart of your heart.

There was only one way to be happy: to give everything he had, just as she had done.

He had to be willing to die for her. And even more important: live for her.

Choose me. Love me.

This was what love meant. What family meant. It didn't mean requiring someone to jump through hoops. It didn't mean a lifetime of ignoring someone until you found a use for them, as his father had done. It didn't mean abandoning them when you had a better offer, as Nadia had.

Love meant acceptance. Protection. It meant a lifetime of loyalty through good times and bad.

Love that will last for the rest of my life.

It meant forever.

Santiago sucked in his breath. Belle was his true family. She was his love.

And right now, Belle was in New York. In labor with their baby. Utterly alone.

Turning sharply, he checked for his wallet. He had his passport. He said, "I have to go."

"But—where are you going?" Nadia sounded utterly bewildered. "What about your father's press conference tomorrow?"

"Tell him to forget it."

"You're leaving us?"

Santiago looked at Nadia one last time. "I'm sorry. I don't really care about you, or the old man, either. Be honest. Neither of you really care about me. You ignored me until you had a use for me."

"But you're supposed to be the heir," she wailed. "You're supposed to make me a duchess!"

He snorted, shaking his head. "Tell my father that if he wants an heir, I recommend he marry you himself."

Leaving her behind, Santiago left the castle of Sangovia for good.

He was done with his old childish dreams. There was only one dream he wanted now. One dream that was real, and for that, he would risk everything he had. Heart and soul.

* * *

"Just a little longer…" her friend Letty pleaded.

Belle panted for breath, choked with tears of pain as the contraction finally ended. Stretched out in bed in the private room in the hospital, her legs beneath a blanket, she'd wanted to be brave, so she'd told the doctors she didn't need an epidural. It was a choice she was now sorely regretting.

The labor had already lasted for hours and hours, and it still wasn't time to push. Her daughter, after demanding to be born early, was suddenly taking her time.

"You're doing fine," Letty said, letting go of her hand with a wince, to reach for a cup of ice chips.

Belle took the cup gratefully and sucked on an ice chip, thirsty and exhausted in this brief respite between contractions. She knew that soon, the pain would start again, and hurt so much throughout her body that if she'd had anything left in her stomach, she would have thrown up.

"Thanks for being here with me," she whispered. "I just hope I didn't break your hand."

"It's fine," her friend said, stretching her hand gingerly. Her eyes narrowed. "It's nothing compared to how my hand will hurt after the next time I see Santiago's face. After what he did to you… The bastard! The total bastard!"

"Don't talk about him that way," Belle said weakly as she started to feel the beginnings of the next contraction. "He tried his…best. He couldn't…love me. So he let me go…"

They both turned their heads as they heard some kind of commotion in the hospital hallway, outside the door. It was loud enough to be heard over the medical equipment monitoring her heartbeat and the baby's with beeps and lights.

"What on earth…?" With a frown, the nurse who'd been hovering by Belle's bed went out to check, closing the door behind her.

But the noise only increased. Clutching her belly, Belle panted, "Go see what's happening."

"I'm not leaving you," Letty said stoutly.

"Any…distraction…is better…"

With a reluctant nod, Letty went out into the hall.

And then the yelling really started. For a moment, Belle lost track of her labor pains in her sudden fear that World War III had just started in the hospital hallway.

The shouting abruptly stopped. The door exploded open to reveal the last person she'd expected to see. Standing in the doorway was Santiago, tall and broad-shouldered, his dark eyes bright.

Was she dreaming? Had she died?

As the pain started to crest, she stretched out her hand to him with a choked gasp, and in two seconds, he crossed to her side, putting his hand in hers. With him there, though the pain was worse than ever, suddenly she felt stronger and braver, and knew she could endure. With his hand in hers, she knew she could squeeze as hard as she wanted, and it wouldn't hurt him. She didn't have to hold back. So she didn't. Clutching his hand tight, she screamed through the pain.

When the contraction finally was over, he had tears in his eyes. She was shocked.

"Did I hurt your hand?" she said anxiously.

"My hand?" he looked down at it in bewilderment, then shook his head. "It's fine."

"Then why—"

"Forgive me," he choked out.

Then to her astonished eyes, Santiago fell to his knees beside the hospital bed, next to the blanket that covered her legs. He looked up, his dark eyes searing her soul.

"I was a coward," he whispered. "Afraid to admit what was in my heart. I thought I could send you away and stay safe and numb the rest of my life. I can't." He set his jaw. "I won't."

"What are you saying?" she croaked out.

"You are everything I was ever afraid to want. Everything good. Everything I thought I didn't deserve. I need you, Belle." He took a deep breath. "I love you."

She gaped down at him. "I thought you could only love Nadia…"

"Nadia?" He snorted. "She was a trophy. Like art on my wall or a million-acre ranch. You are no man's trophy, Belle."

Her heart fell. She bit her lip. "No. I'm not."

"You're no trophy," he said in a low, intense voice, "because you're far more. You are my woman. My equal partner. My better half. My love. And if you'll have me," he said humbly, "my wife."

She sucked in her breath. "Your—"

Then the new contraction hit, and she reached desperately for his hand. Rising to his feet, he took it immediately, holding it close, against his heart. The pain built sharply, leaving her gasping for breath.

For what seemed like hours, he held her hand unflinchingly, speaking to her in Spanish and English, calming her with his deep voice, giving her his strength, helping her through the pain. As the contraction finally subsided, the nurse checked her beneath the blanket, then gave a quick nod. "I'm going to get the doctor."

Belle and Santiago were alone. She took a deep breath.

"Thank you," she whispered. "For being here. For our baby."

His expression turned sad. "Just for the baby?" he said slowly. "It's too late, isn't it? I've hurt you too badly to ever hope for forgiveness…"

She said in a trembling voice, "Do you really love me?"

Sudden, shocked hope lit his dark eyes.

"With everything I have. Everything I am. I love you." Leaning over the hospital bed, he kissed her sweaty forehead tenderly. "Love me," he whispered. "Forgive me. Marry me."

Belle wondered if she was dreaming. Then she decided she didn't care. "Yes."

He drew back, looking down at her with joy. "You'll marry me?"

Wordlessly, she nodded. Rushing to fling open the door, he called two people inside: a man dressed in a plain black suit and Letty, following behind, holding a bag from the hospital gift shop.

"This is John Alvarez, the hospital pastor," Santiago told her. "He's going to marry us."

Her jaw dropped. "Right now?"

"What, are you busy?" he teased.

She snorted, then grew serious. "But…what about the big wedding you wanted?"

"We already have a license. I don't want to live another moment without you as my wife." He cupped her cheek. "I love you, Belle."

A slow-rising smile lifted her lips.

"I love you too," she whispered, tears falling down her face unheeded. Pulling on his hand, she brought him closer to the hospital bed and kissed him, laughing her happiness. Then she groaned, as she felt the next contraction begin to rise. "But we'd better do this fast."

And so it was that, plain gold bands from the hospital gift shop were slipped within minutes on both their hands, and they were declared man and wife. And just in time.

"Anyone that's not family, get out!" the nurse said, shooing the pastor and Letty into the hallway. In that moment, the doctor hurried into the room.

"All right, Belle," the doctor said, smiling. "Are you ready to push?"

Forty-five minutes later, their daughter, named Emma Jamie Velazquez after the baby's grandmother and grandfather, was brought into this world. A short while later, as Belle watched her husband—her *husband!*—hold their daughter, who was a fat eight pounds ten ounces, tenderly in his arms, she was overwhelmed with happiness.

"Someone wants to meet you," Santiago said, smiling, and gently placed their newborn daughter in Belle's arms.

As she looked down at their precious baby, the miracle she'd once thought she could never have, tears fell from Belle's eyes that she didn't even try to hide. She whispered, "She's so beautiful."

"Like her mother," Santiago said. Leaning down, he kissed her forehead with infinite tenderness, then kissed their sleeping baby's. He looked down at Belle—his *wife*—in the hospital bed. "I love you, Mrs. Velazquez."

She caught her breath at hearing her name for the first time.

Letty peeked around the door into the room to make sure it was safe, then entered, beaming at the baby before she turned to Santiago. "Um, you forgive me for slapping you earlier, right? I feel kind of bad about it now."

"I had it coming," Santiago said, adjusting his jaw a little ruefully. "Thanks for helping with the rings."

Letty grinned. "No problem. It was easy. It was either gold bands or the candy ones. Hey, you two lovebirds, there was one part of the wedding the pastor had to cut when we got kicked out." Letty looked between them. "You may now kiss the bride."

Santiago looked down at Belle with a gleam in his black eyes. "The perfect end to a perfect day."

Belle smiled through her tears.

Once, she'd thought that all her chances for love and happiness had passed her by. She'd thought that her choice to take care of her brothers instead of herself, to sacrifice her own dreams for others, meant that she'd ended her own chance for a bright future.

Now she realized that life wasn't like that.

Every day could be a new start. Every day could be a fresh miracle. And today, the first day of their marriage, the first day of her daughter's life, she knew it wasn't the end of anything. As her husband lowered his head to kiss her in a private vow that would last the rest of their lives, she knew it was all just beginning.

Santiago got married in a quick hospital ceremony just minutes before his baby was born, and his two best friends never let him forget it.

"And you said you'd never get married in some tacky quick wedding," said Darius Kyrillos, who'd married at City Hall.

"You said you'd never get married at all," said his friend Kassius Black, who'd wed at an over-the-top grand ceremony in New Orleans.

Santiago grinned. "A man can change his mind, can't he?"

He was on his third helping of Texas-style barbecue, and the three men were sitting across a huge sofa in a corner of the ballroom of his Upper East Side mansion. Officially, it was a party to celebrate the christening of six-week-old Emma. Unofficially, it was also a wedding reception. The house was crowded, decidedly a family affair filled with friends and relatives, including Belle's two brothers who'd come up to New York for the event, and neighbors, employees and their families. For dinner, they'd had champagne, beer, barbecue, corn on the cob and homemade ice cream. It was November, the time of Thanksgiving. But Belle had definite ideas about how she wanted this party to be.

"Fun like home," she'd said with a grin.

So there was a bluegrass band playing, to the mild shock

of the foreign dignitaries that had been invited. But they seemed to like it, and even strangers had become friends, with people dancing and kids running around. And did he actually see someone's golden retriever running madly across the house…?

The only family not in attendance was his father, the Duke of Sangovia, who had recently, and rather shockingly, wed his former daughter-in-law, the famous movie star. Another marriage "partnership." Santiago shuddered thinking of it. And those were the people he might have spent his life with, like a prison sentence, if Belle hadn't saved him. If she hadn't taught him to be brave enough to risk his heart and soul.

If she hadn't taught him what love actually meant.

Now, as the three husbands sat together, drinking frosty mugs of beer and watching the crowd, Santiago looked down at his daughter, who'd fallen asleep in his arms. After six weeks, he was starting to feel like a pro as a dad.

Kassius and Darius, who'd also brought their wives and children to the party, looked down at the fat baby in Santiago's arms.

"Babies are adorable," Kassius said.

"Especially when they're sleeping," Darius said.

"That's what I meant," he said.

"To sleeping babies—" Santiago raised his beer mug "—and beautiful wives." They all clinked glasses. Softly, so as not to wake the baby.

Across the crowd, Santiago saw Belle, and as always, he lost his breath.

She was beautiful—the center of this house as she was the center of his world. Her long dark hair tumbled over her shoulders, over her curvaceous body in the soft red dress. As she felt his glance, their eyes locked across the crowd. Electricity raced through his body.

Santiago had spent his whole childhood dreaming of

having a place in the world. A home. A family. It had come true, just not in the way he'd expected.

He hadn't been born into this family. He'd created it. He and Belle together. From the moment they'd fallen into bed and accidentally conceived a child.

Had it been an accident? he suddenly wondered. Or was it possible he'd always known, from the moment he first met Belle, that she would be the one to break the spell?

Because that was what she'd done. It was funny. Belle had once compared him to a knight, saying he'd slain dragons for Nadia like something out of a fairy tale. But he hadn't. All he'd done was make a lot of money. He'd never risked anything. He'd never saved anyone.

Not like Belle.

She was the true knight. She was the one who'd slain the dragon. She was the one who'd saved his soul. He would always be grateful for that miracle.

Tomorrow, they would leave on a two-month honeymoon—bringing baby Emma, of course—on a trip around the world. Belle had planned this reception, so he'd insisted on organizing the honeymoon. "What are your top five dream travel destinations?"

"Paris," she'd said instantly, then "London." She'd bitten her lip. "The Christmas markets in Germany. The neon lights of Tokyo. Or maybe—" she'd tilted her head "—a beach vacation in Australia? The Great Barrier Reef?" With a sigh, she'd shaken her head. "I'm glad I'm not the one who has to decide!"

But as it turned out neither did he. Because they were going to see everything. Emma would be a very well-traveled baby before she even had her first bite of baby food.

Their family would see the world together, all of them for the first time. It would all be new to Santiago, too. Because this time, he'd be leading with his heart.

In the ballroom, Belle came up to the sofa, smiling. "You boys having fun?"

"Yes," they all said cheerily, and in Kassius's and Darius's case a little tipsily. Belle grinned at Santiago.

"Want to help cut the cake?"

"Absolutely." He rose to his feet, their sleeping baby still tucked securely against his chest. With his free hand, he suddenly pulled his wife close and kissed her. Not a little kiss, either. He kissed her long and hard, until they started getting catcalls and whistles and cheers from the guests, and he felt her tremble in his arms.

She drew back, her eyes big. "What was that for?"

"It's the start of a whole life loving you," he whispered, cupping her cheek. "I wanted to do it right."

Belle leaned her head against his shoulder, and for a moment, the three of them stood nestled together. Then they heard someone yell, "Come quick! The kids are coming at the cake with spoons, and there's a dog close behind!"

Laughing, Santiago and Belle, with their sleeping baby, went to cut the cake. And as they were toasted and cheered by their family and friends, he looked down tenderly at his wife, who smiled back at him, her eyes shining with love. And Santiago knew, for the first time in his life, that he was finally home.

* * * * *

If you enjoyed
CARRYING THE SPANIARD'S CHILD
by Jennie Lucas
why not explore these other
SECRET HEIRS OF BILLIONAIRES
themed stories?

THE DESERT KING'S SECRET HEIR
by Annie West
THE SHEIKH'S SECRET SON
by Maggie Cox
THE INNOCENT'S SHAMEFUL SECRET
by Sara Craven
THE GREEK'S PLEASURABLE REVENGE
by Andie Brock
THE SECRET KEPT FROM THE GREEK
by Susan Stephens

Available now!

MILLS & BOON®

MODERN™

POWER, PASSION AND IRRESISTIBLE TEMPTATION

MILLS & BOON®

EXCLUSIVE EXTRACT

Natasha Pellegrini and Matteo Manaserro's reunion catches them both in a potent mix of emotion, and they surrender to their explosive passion. Natasha was a virgin until Matteo's touch branded her as his and when Matteo discovers Natasha is pregnant, he's intent on claiming his baby. Except he hasn't bargained on their insatiable chemistry binding them together so completely!

Read on for a sneak preview of Michelle Smart's book
CLAIMING HIS ONE-NIGHT BABY
The second part of her Bound to a Billionaire trilogy

'For better or worse we're going to be tied together by our child for the rest of our lives and the only way we're going to get through it is by always being honest with each other. We will argue and disagree but you must always speak the truth to me.'

Natasha fought to keep her feet grounded and her limbs from turning into fondue but it was a fight she was losing, Matteo's breath warm on her face, his thumb gently moving on her skin but scorching it, the heat from his body almost penetrating her clothes, heat crawling through her, pooling in her most intimate place.

His scent was right there too, filling every part of her, and she wanted to bury her nose into his neck and inhale him.

She'd kissed him without any thought, a desperate compulsion to touch him and comfort him flooding her, and then the fury had struck from nowhere, all her private thoughts about the direction he'd taken his career in converging to realise he'd thrown it all away in the pursuit of riches.

And now she wanted to kiss him again.

As if he could sense the need inside her, he brought his mouth close to hers but not quite touching, the promise of a kiss.

'And now I will ask you something and I want complete honesty,' he whispered, the movement of his words making his lips dance against hers like a breath.

The fluttering of panic sifted into the compulsive desire. She hated lies too. She never wanted to tell another, especially not to him. But she had to keep her wits about her because there were things she just could not tell because no matter what he said about lies always being worse, sometimes it was the truth that could destroy a life.

But, God, how could she think properly when her head was turning into candyfloss at his mere touch?

His other hand trailed down her back and clasped her bottom to pull her flush to him. Her abdomen clenched to feel his erection pressing hard against her lower stomach. His lips moved lightly over hers, still tantalising her with the promise of his kiss. 'Do you want me to let you go?'

Her hands that she'd clenched into fists at her sides to stop from touching him back unfurled themselves and inched to his hips.

The hand stroking her cheek moved round her head and speared her hair. 'Tell me.' His lips found her exposed neck and nipped gently at it. 'Do you want me to stop?'

'Matteo…' Finally, she found her voice.

'Yes, *bella*?'

'Don't stop.'

MILLS & BOON ®

Why shop at millsandboon.co.uk?

Each year, thousands of romance readers
find their perfect read at millsandboon.co.uk.
That's because we're passionate about
bringing you the very best romantic fiction.
Here are some of the advantages of
shopping at www.millsandboon.co.uk:

* **Get new books first**—you'll be able to buy
  your favourite books one month before they
  hit the shops

* **Get exclusive discounts**—you'll also be
  able to buy our specially created monthly
  collections, with up to 50% off the RRP

* **Find your favourite authors**—latest news,
  interviews and new releases for all your
  favourite authors and series on our website,
  plus ideas for what to try next

* **Join in**—once you've bought your favourite
  books, don't forget to register with us to rate,
  review and join in the discussions

Visit **www.millsandboon.co.uk**
for all this and more today!